BY THE SAME AUTHOR

With Malice Toward Some

Margaret Halsey

SOME OF MY BEST FRIENDS ARE SOLDIERS

A Kind of Novel

Simon and Schuster, New York, 1944

ABOUT THE APPEARANCE OF BOOKS IN WARTIME

A recent ruling by the War Production Board has curtailed the use of paper by book publishers in 1944.

In line with this ruling and in order to conserve materials and manpower, we are co-operating by:

1. Using lighter-weight paper, which reduces the bulk of our books substantially.
2. Printing books with smaller margins and with more words to each page. Result: fewer pages per book.

Slimmer and smaller books will save paper and plate metal and labor. We are sure that readers will understand the publishers' desire to co-operate as fully as possible with the objectives of the War Production Board and our government.

MANUFACTURED IN THE UNITED STATES OF AMERICA
AMERICAN BOOK—STRATFORD PRESS, INC., NEW YORK

To M. R. S.
from the Mrs.

At the representation of my publishers, who think no grind-stone is half so pretty as when it has got my nose next to it, I have gone to the probably unnecessary trouble of making up all these places and people out of my head.

M. H.

Dear Jeff,

I'm sorry I cried when you left for the induction center, but it was your fault. Customarily, you look like a lady novelist's stereotype of the cool young scientist, so it jolted me into tears when I saw you standing there so unscientifically lonely and scared. It reminded me of when you recited *Trees* for Arbor Day in the eighth grade, and I sat in the back of the room with the sixth grade and promised God the entire solar system if He would let you get through it without getting stuck. At the moment, I wish I hadn't bargained so spaciously, because now He has the solar system and I have nothing left to trade for your safe return.

I make no pretense of not being upset by your departure, but Father is taking it with what he considers stoic calm. Father's stoic calms are all right, if you remember to negotiate them with bare masts and the

I

helmsman lashed to the wheel. First he couldn't find his pipe, and we went through the house like the hounds of spring on winter's traces before we finally located it. Then he came into the kitchen and wanted some more breakfast. I had gotten the food put away and was just starting to wash the dishes, so this request did not produce in me a great surge of filial affection. However, I made him a cup of Ovaltine, and after drinking half of it, he went into his room and opened and closed the desk drawers for about ten minutes. Emerging, he announced that the house was stuffy, and trailed around opening windows to the benevolent air of midwinter. Altogether, he was about as imperturbable as a nymphomaniac in Carnival time.

The last thing was that he came into the kitchen again and said he wasn't going to rent your room and have any damned, intrusive stranger stalking around the apartment, even if we starved to death.

"All right," I said patiently. "We'll have ham sandwiches for dinner. Under glass."

He looked ashamed and put his arm around me so roughly that it left dents in my bones. One of the many reasons I'm sorry Mother died so young is that I'd like to have asked her what Father was like at the age of twenty-five. It's presumptuous of anybody's parents ever to have been young (after all, who do they think they are, human beings?); but Mother's must have been the original of all those courtships subsequently known as "whirlwind."

It being too early to go to the office, the Progenitor

went for a walk. From the way he settled into his coat, it was clear that he felt he'd borne up under saying good-bye to you with something really flashy in the way of composure.

I feel awful myself about having someone in your room; but it will be better than moving. You'll be able to visualize us at our accustomed occupations. Not, of course, that there's any faster way to bring a housewife to her knees than saddling her with an apartment in a remodeled brownstone. Since you left, the hot water faucet in the bathroom basin has stopped working. The superintendent, when this lapse was pointed out to him, was indignant that we had even mentioned the matter. The faucet may not be working, but the leak in my bedroom ceiling is still working like a beaver. The superintendent feels that as long as water enters the apartment somehow, we have no call to be so finicking about the manner of its arrival.

I like our place of residence, though. I went up to see Janie and the baby this afternoon and thought, as I always think, that compared to our fireplaces, tall ceilings and career-diplomat woodwork, Janie's run-of-the-mill apartment is very prosy and uncaptivating. I concede that Janie's doorbell works and ours doesn't. I spoke to the superintendent about the doorbell again this morning, but he still thinks electricity is something you fetch from the sky with a kite and he intimated that my request was distinctly unreasonable.

What I started to say was that I went up to see Janie, and you'll be glad to hear that the infant Deb-

3

orah has not relaxed her devastating grip upon the heartstrings. Just in the little time since you saw her, she's learned to walk all by herself. She still handles her feet as if they were the last thing in the world she'd expected to find on the end of her legs, but she doesn't let them hamper her. She gets into everything. While Janie and I were talking this afternoon, she went into the kitchen and took a small, round bite out of every apple and potato in the vegetable bin. We didn't know what was happening until she came off a bad second with the onions.

Janie has got her semi-housebroken. That is to say, she knows that with the advent of certain agreeable colonic sensations, she is supposed to say, "Potty." But she hasn't yet learned that it isn't usual to let 'er rip until one is strategically disposed upon a bit of plumbing. You would laugh to see our ordinarily lethargic sister when she hears those ominous syllables. Among the many beautiful qualities developed by motherhood is a fast start in a sprint.

I must bring this to a close, Skipper, because this is a Canteen night. Eight of the fifty Junior Hostesses whose destinies I am supposed to keep within reasonable bounds are down with colds, and six more have called up with excuses markedly deficient in narrative power, so I shall be shorthanded again. It's a chronic condition when you have to deal with volunteer war workers. They aren't paid, so one has no hold over them except their own consciences—which, in some cases, are not exactly curved to fit the palm. However,

I always love going over to the Canteen, even though there are times when, in point of ease, peace and serenity, a person would be better off on the reef of Norman's Woe.

We're waiting eagerly, of course, to hear where they send you. And I want to know how you feel—not only physically, but also your curly little psyche. I hope you aren't too much confused and upset and trod-upon. Soldiers have told me that the first few days in the Army have even thin red lines of heroes hanging on the ropes, and your native pugnacity has always been directed into intellectual channels. I don't know whether it's any comfort to you—puzzling over which part of the body, if any, is supposed to go into a G. I. shoe—but I'm awfully proud of having a brother in the Army. "*That* will show the enemy!" I think, looking them right in the eye and preening.

With which irrational but stimulating sentiment, I close. Write to us as soon as you can. It's lonely around here, now that the minstrel boy to the wars has gone.

Love,
Gretchen

January 6th

Dear Jeff,

Whenever I remember that I'm twenty-six years old—a recollection that assails me entirely too often—I get an unlovely sensation of being past my prime;

5

but the greedy years do have a curious way of dissolving long-standing tensions. The other day, when I was up at Janie's, we were reminiscing about our childhood. The slant of Janie's remarks suddenly made me realize, to my great astonishment, that as a little girl, Janie always felt left out of things. You and I were older and—shall we not be squeamish?—brighter. We had a closed corporation, with Father calling us I Am and Me Too, while Janie was left sitting alone among her naturally curly hair. But Janie's feeling still seems a little unreal to me. I've always had to scrape the bottom of the pot for crumbled compliments like "piquant"—which is just a compressed way of telling a woman she might as well be a good sport about it—whereas Janie has spent her whole life making all the other females in sight look as if they'd just come in on a breeches buoy.

What more could a person have wanted? Much as I loved and cherished being your favorite, I would always have given you away to the junkman if, by so doing, I could have looked like Janie.

But now I'm not so sure (you'll be relieved to know). Janie gets everything she wants in life merely by holding still and letting one breath succeed another in her flawlessly sculptured nostrils. It cuts her off from the rest of us—who achieve our ends, if at all, only by struggling like locomotives on a three-in-one grade. I suppose that's why Bill and Janie are so happy together. Bill hears people say his wife is beautiful, but it has no meaning to him. He hasn't seen the

6

woman yet who can compare in sensual pleasure with the principle of the suspension bridge. He loves Janie because she's sweet-tempered, which I suppose is why she married him in preference to one of the more spectacular candidates. Well, there's one nice thing about Janie: Her family will never have to live through any more weeks like the ones which succeeded the announcement of her engagement. It was a poor day, then, which didn't produce its Beau Gesture, and the Foreign Legion must have felt like those people who have suddenly begun to use the right deodorant.

I'm not going to be falsely rhetorical and ask how I got started on the subject of our sister. I embarked on it because I've been thinking about it for the last few days. But even your limitless patience with me is probably not equal to any further reflections, so I'll only add that in the last analysis, I'm glad I was the one who had the inside track with Brother Geoffrey. Please, may I have your autograph? On my bifocals, if you don't mind.

Of course, what you really want in this letter is news from home, but you haven't been away long enough for any to accumulate. The house seems very empty without you—surprisingly so, considering how sound-less and subdued you've been the last year. Miss Ellsworth called up to ask if I had your address yet. She's knitting you a pair of socks. Miss E. is so stainlessly secretarial that it's hard to picture her knitting, but they'll probably be the best socks you've ever ruined in half a day by not cutting your toenails. Miss Adel-

7

man and Miss Stafford are also formulating socks and a sweater, respectively, in your behalf.

The Daydreaming Department at the lab is, I'm afraid, down by the bow on account of your absence. I feel deeply sympathetic, though it always gives me a mild shock when I talk to Miss Ellsworth and Friends. No degree of familiarity could ever make me contemptuous of your nice, sleek hair and well-shaped head, but to me you're just a little old sibling I got from Sears, Roebuck, and if I were being mercilessly truthful, I'd describe you as being built like a plucked hawk. Miss E., however, for all her imposing correctness, would think me treasonable if I suggested that there are one or two minor points by which I can distinguish you from Henry Fonda.

I had a letter from one of my Junior Hostesses this morning who wants to resign from the Canteen. She's a lovely-looking child of nineteen with an air of great tranquillity on top and a good deal of emotional intensity underneath. Her family had a felicitous premonition and christened her Pamela, which suits her exactly. At any rate, Pamela is angered and confused by the Canteen's split personality. The Columbus Circle Canteen has been publicized from here to the rings of Saturn as an organization manned by celebrities, eminences, and Week-end Specials in colossi, whereas actually it is kept running, day in and day out, by (for the most part) agreeable people who are only household words in the sense that they are called Mother or Sis. The people with the resounding names

8

don't come in except to get their pictures taken.

In fervent, if somewhat undisciplined prose, Pamela points out that the colossi are using the Canteen—and, by implication, the war itself—for personal publicity, without kicking in anything in return. Pamela's best beau is out at sea, where he tucks shells into a gun during that far from dreamy interval after the fuse is cut. Pamela, therefore, has rather rigid notions about the word "service," and burns with resentment at seeing it debauched by a group of self-dramatizing punks. (My words, not hers.)

Lord knows, I see her point, having gone through the same thing myself in the beginning. I called her up and said that though the present setup isn't right, nothing is going to be any righter if nobody works at the Canteen at all and the servicemen have to hang around the streets because there aren't enough places for them to go. I also expressed some sentiments about not having tyrannical standards of perfection, because they carry within them the seeds of their own defeat. I can only hope her intuition didn't reveal to her that on the subject of where to compromise with evil, Momma is far from feeling as authoritative as she sounds.

As a matter of fact, when our little oasis on 59th Street first opened, all the literary, social, financial and artistic geniuses in the city really did work there. Only when it shook down into a moderately routinized operation, most of the geniuses slipped out through the interstices. And it's really better that way. When

9

you want sandwiches made, the logical people to make them are women who are used to making sandwiches. The physical and mental glamour girls are apt to be a mite overtrained. Just the same, I wish we weren't wearing borrowed plumes. A volunteer organization is by nature manic-depressive, and it makes things awfully complicated when it has schizophrenia as well.

Am I rambling on too long, Jeff? I have a whole hour with nothing to do—or, at least, nothing will happen if I refrain from doing anything—and I'm apt to wax talkative on the subject of the Junior Hostesses. They don't have, as outsiders generally assume, a very romantic job. Most servicemen fail to resemble the pictures in the War Bond posters (or do I have to tell you?). The Canteen is small and hot, and the dance floor cannot compete in charm and appeal with a jungle, because a jungle stands still. Some of our guests have looked upon the wine when it was red, and others remember, from their early religious training, only the line about male and female created He them. The balance, which is also the majority, are so shy that a lady could make rather more headway with a lockjaw patient. To the business of entertaining these impetuous and unimpetuous males, the Junior Hostesses bring only what wisdom and experience of life they have been able to pile up in about two decades. It's amazing—and, of course, thoroughly heart-warming—to see how some of them have developed since they started to work at the Canteen. Not only do they acquire poise and tolerance, but they get adjusted to,

and even acquire a taste for, the dizzying multitudi-
nousness of democracy.

Reading over the above paragraph, I see that in
mentioning the occupational risks of being a Junior
Hostess, I left out the most terrifying one of all—Mrs.
Alicia Sadler. I don't believe I've spoken of Mrs.
Sadler before, have I? She's one of the few socialites
who work regularly at the Canteen, and the prevailing
sentiment is that it would be a fine thing if she would
go back to baby farming, or body snatching, or whatever it was she did before the war. However, she's on
the Canteen Governing Board, so I guess the road
winds uphill all the way, yes, to the very end.

At a distance, the formidable Alicia seems all benevolence. She's an old lady with high-piled white hair
and an addiction to snowy fichus and amethyst-and-
seed-pearl jewelry. It's only when you get closer that
you see she has the eyes and nose of an eagle and the
bearing of a constipated Empress. She considers the
servicemen her social inferiors, and takes pains to
make them aware of it. She orders them to eat, she
orders them to sit down, she orders them to dance, and
then if she doesn't like their dancing, she orders them
to stop. Technically, she's a Senior Hostess, but though
she's unquestionably senior, I've seen children starv-
ing in the streets who wouldn't call her a hostess.

Compared to the Junior Hostesses, though, the servicemen get off easy. Mrs. Sadler, viewing Saint Ce-
cilia at the organ, could find half a dozen ways in
which that estimable female was unladylike and sex-

ridden, so you can imagine how much chance the Junior Hostesses have. The worst of it is that Mrs. S. makes a point of voicing her strictures where all the surrounding servicemen can't help hearing. My Junior Hostesses come to me in tears, but there's nothing I can do. Mrs. Sadler is rich, and she has rich friends, and they all give donations to the Canteen. We have been specifically instructed not to get embroiled with her, an injunction which makes sense in every way but one—it ought not to be issued to organisms composed of flesh and blood.

Well, fellow, I only started this letter in an effort to tide you over until news and drama develop on the home front, such as Aunt Julie keeping something on her stomach or our treasured cousin G. discovering that he's come out with his wallet and doesn't need to borrow five dollars. As a correspondent, I seem to have contracted middle-aged spread. But it's been a long time since we sat up late talking and having a meeting of the minds. I think about you a lot, and I hope your head is unbowed. (I know it's bloody.) Do please try, darling, not to be too tense. After all, when you relax, you can see that a sergeant is only a man who accepts cash money for behaving just like Father.

Love,
Gretchen

Beloved Soiviceman—

(I heard a gateman in Grand Central pronouncing it that way, while shepherding you fellers in ahead of the civilians, and it haunts me.)

I'm terribly sorry it's Fort Bragg. I'd been hoping it would be Meade or Belvoir or one of those places where you might once in a while be able to get home for the week end. I hear at the Canteen that the citizens of Fayetteville have approximately the same attitude toward the military as Mrs. Sadler—with the additional advantage of being in a position to over-charge them for everything. I am sending you a box with some razor blades, cigarettes, gum, Pocket Books, and other commodities designed to shake the foundations of free enterprise in North Carolina. I'm sorry the box isn't big enough to include a pretty girl and a contingent of rum cokes.

But there's no use putting ideas in your head, for I gather that Bragg isn't Venusberg, or even Luna Park. By way of distraction, in case I've started you on ener-vating and unsuitable trains of thought, I'd like to enter a complaint—to wit, that your letters, darling, are heartlessly noncommittal and don't tell me any-thing. Not anything that really counts, anyway. You had prunes for breakfast. I happen to know that you used to think prunes represented caloric intake in its least seductive form, but perhaps Army life has made you so hungry that you cannot shovel prunes down fast enough. Or maybe the prunes will prove to be the raditional straw that broke, etc. Please don't be a deserter, pal. I won't have any place to put the summer blankets if I have to hide you in the cedar chest.

But why am I beating about the bush? What I really want to do is read you a lecture. (I don't have to take my courage in both hands. There's only enough of it to fill one.) Jeff, I think your grief about Ellen has gone on too long. When you stopped playing tennis, which was the one non-scientific thing you were good at, I didn't say anything. When you stopped seeing people, I kept my mouth shut, though I wanted to take you by the scruff of the neck and rub your nose in a May-pole dance. I refrained from comment when you worked so late every night that all I ever saw of you was sandwich crusts on the kitchen table when I went in to start the breakfast. This monumental silence I was able to accomplish because I knew you were going into the Army and that straightforward institution, I thought, would do a little rough surgery on your circular melancholy.

But so far as I can tell, the Army doesn't even make you mad, and this worries me. If you're treating Fort Bragg to a tableau of the Sleeping Beauty, you're not only going to have no fun in large quantities yourself, but you're also going to give rise to many sensations of acute distaste in the manly bosoms surrounding you. You see, honeybunch, you intellectual gents have a notion you discharge your full responsibility to your fellow men by going to a laboratory and inventing benign serums. But you don't. Because where does

14

that leave me? Sitting around alone, not having diseases.

Part of that responsibility has to be discharged in person. To me, for instance. To the guys juxtaposed to you in the Army. (If there *are* any guys juxtaposed to you in the Army. For all I can tell from your letters, you may be in solitary confinement.) That's why I'd feel much better if you were writing me the sort of letters you used to send when you were in Europe. Why don't you leave the communiqués to the General Staff? They get paid for it.

But I'm too scared to go on. It's the first time in my life I've ever criticized you for anything more serious than steaming up the bathroom so that my organdy curtains wilted, and I'm unsure of myself in the role of His Majesty's Loyal Opposition. I really am worried about you, though.

If you're not too angry with me to read further, I'll see what I can scrape up in the way of news from Fort 273 East 49th Street.

I've had a gratifying triumph over the superintendent. This morning while I was leaning on my oil mop and dreamily listening to a soap opera, I heard a tremendous pounding and calling down at the street door. The accents were familiar, and I realized at once that the super had come to fix the furnace and had forgotten his keys. Everybody in the building was out except me, and our doorbell was out of order.

I gave him a full minute to get worked up to concert pitch, then opened the front window and leaned out.

"Did you want something?" I asked sweetly.

"Wanna get in," he said, the superfluousness of the statement being evident even to his dim mind.

"Why didn't you call me on the telephone?" I said. "That, at least, still works."

I went downstairs and let him in, and he disappeared through the cellar door with more dispatch than I have ever seen him show in the execution of his duties. There wasn't even a trace of his customary maddening shuffle. This afternoon he turned up with a new battery and fixed the doorbell.

As a matter of fact, I wasn't really leaning dreamily on my oil mop when the superintendent erupted, because with a six-room apartment and no maid, the opportunities for dreaming are intermittent, to say the least. I don't, though, miss Coline nearly as much as I expected to. It's nice to be alone in the apartment, and to be free to pursue my duties in paint-stained old slacks and with my hair pinned up in those damp lumps which, cocoon-like, precede the springing curls. Coline always expected me to look like A Perfect Little Lady, and I was too weak in the character to let her see that the obligation was sometimes oppressive. As I am now, I don't exactly bring an evil gleam into the eyes of the exterminator, but after all, in his business, he must see much worse things than me.

I don't have to worry about impressing the window cleaner, because it's impossible to get one any more. I cleaned the windows myself yesterday. I love doing the insides, but I'm so frightened of sitting out on the

16

sill to do the outsides that my hands shake and I keep letting the cloths fall—though it isn't really much of a drop. I tried to hearten myself by reflecting that it was a mere nothing compared to what the paratroops do. But when I told this to Father, thinking to impress him with my bravery, he remarked coldly that the parachute troops have parachutes, and I'd better just let the windows get dirty. I realized too late that I shouldn't have mentioned it to him at all. It irks him that he can't do it himself, but if he were to get a heart attack in mid-air, it would complicate things. To say the least.

However, it was my original intention to record the fact that we are getting along surprisingly well without Coline. The house doesn't have that gleaming, shining look it used to have when Coline was wearing everything to a nubbin with her scrubbing and polishing. In fact, people look at our brass fire irons and say, "My, what lovely pewter!" And the candlesticks. It never seemed to me before that we had a particularly lavish endowment of candlesticks, but now that I have to clean them, I begin to think Mother and Father, when they married, intended to set up housekeeping in a cathedral. These details, however, are not the sort which ever caught your eye, and come to think of it, I guess this is one paragraph that is going to leave you completely unmoved.

There is only one wartime inconvenience—I decided this morning—by which I am really pierced to the heart, and that is having to wear rayon stockings instead of nylon. Rayon stockings feel as if you had painted molasses on your legs and it was slowly running down. They bunch on the foot, giving you the distinct sensation of walking around on a couple of unmade beds. My brother Geoffrey, from whom I used to take a good deal of what is known as lip, always said I was vain about my legs; but with the advent of rayon, a lot of my complacent exhibitionism withered on the vine.

Speaking of inconveniences, the hot water faucet in the bathroom still isn't working, and this morning the cold water was apparently being piped in directly from the Black Sea. The superintendent came with a long piece of wire, which he introduced into the pipes somewhat in the manner of a doctor treating a sinus patient. This restored the cold water to its original purity, but the hot water still remains in a cataleptic trance. Ah, well, man wants but little here below. I myself have only one, teeny, miniscule requirement: Some day I want to live in a house where the plumbing wouldn't be regarded with disdain by Pocahontas.

So far we haven't rented your room. There have been six people to look at it, and I'm happy to say that all of them exclaimed instantly how handsome it was. I did so much sewing and scraping and painting and trudging around to make that little grotto presentable—without, at the same time, spending more than I could raise on old club soda bottles—that I melt like chocolate in a baby's hand when I hear it praised. Of the six people who came to see it, four were pleasant persons I would have liked to have had here. Unfortunately, they didn't think they could pay what we were asking. The other two candidates, though, were so awful I stalled them off.

Of course, it was the awful ones who had plenty of money and didn't object to the price. One was a short, plump, bald young man whose round green eyes and curly little mouth were set in a face which otherwise resembled, in all important particulars, a baking powder biscuit. I had to leave him in the living room while I dealt with the laundryman, and when I came back he was standing next to the table where my typewriter is with his hands behind his back and his head bowed. But not in prayer. He was reading a letter from you that I'd left lying open on the table. I hope it gave him granulated eyelids.

"If you're ready," I said, "we'll look at the room."

He was flustered, but only for a minute. He kept going round and round your room, plucking at the doors, hefting the ornaments, and exclaiming, "What a layout! What a layout!"

He said he was a writer, and he talked a lot about how easy it would be for him to work in such an atmosphere. After a while it began to dawn on him that I was responding about as visibly as Mount Everest under a geologist's hammer, and he left rather abruptly. I didn't ask him his name, so I don't know what he writes, but I do not imagine it is in the tradition of Henry James.

The other awful one was a discontented-looking

woman of about thirty-five whose bleached hair went oddly with a face reminiscent of an old saddle. Her manners were something in which she must have been personally tutored by the guards in a German prison camp. She didn't bother to look at me when she spoke, and the general idea seemed to be that people who have to rent out a room are the social equivalent of carrion.

I didn't contest this point of view. I just stood around reflecting that this, too, would pass. But when she said she would expect the use of the living room to entertain her friends, I was very nearly startled into saying, "Friends? Surely only acquaintances!" I didn't, though. I only said it wouldn't be possible for her to use the living room. She explained impatiently that she'd been in the theater all her life and her friends weren't ordinary people—they were people like Gertrude Lawrence and Helen Hayes. By my calculations, if Saddleface ever entertained the Misses Lawrence and Hayes, it was only by digging a pit in front of the house and covering it with boughs. However, I suppressed this agnostic conclusion and contented myself with replying that Father and I had a policy of not sitting in the kitchen for anyone but Edith Cavell.

At this, Saddleface did a volte-face and turned respectful. She admitted to wanting the room very much, even without the living room. Mendaciously, I said that someone else was interested, too, and I'd have to phone her in the morning. This I did, and luckily was

20

able to leave a message. It was all very unpleasant, but I did get a degree of amusement from thinking about what Father would have done. Father would just have handed her a small white envelope and said, "Here. Have some arsenic."

I saw Philip today (she said, precipitately). He was on the other side of the street, and he didn't see me. It's been about three years, I guess, since the last time I ran across him. Even from across the street, I could tell he was very drunk. Not that he staggered—those chronic alcoholics never do, apparently—but his head was bent and he was looking at the sidewalk in front of him with a terrible, blank, secretive expression, as if he were conducting some sort of horrible revel in the blackest corner of his soul, and didn't want anybody to guess it.

His miraculous good looks—and even you and Father admitted he was two laps ahead of Phoebus Apollo—are almost gone. I wasn't near enough to see his face closely, but he's put on a lot of weight and that lithe, catlike walk he had, which I used to admire so desperately, is spurlos versenkt. It's impossible to realize how many women wanted him eight years ago, and what a conquest I thought it was to marry him. I guess when better houses of cards are built, your sister Gretchen will build them.

What bothers me, Jeff, in the middle of the night, is not that I made an awful mistake at the age of eighteen. Anybody might do that. What unnerves me is that I've nearly made the same kind of catastrophic error several times since. It seems to be a recurring pattern in me. The only men who can turn my blood stream into a condition resembling heavy surf are good-looking heels with characters as intricately unpleasing as the sewers of Paris. With decent and honorable gents, I come all over Platonic. Was ever a woman so perverse and wrongheaded?

Of course, it doesn't make any difference at the moment. Father has a war job which, at his age, he couldn't hold down if I didn't stay at home and take care of him. But what about after the war, when Father has retired and people can get maids again and I won't be so much needed at home? With brown hair, you can't run for Congress.

Oh, well.

The Lord will provide.

If He has all that unreasonable solicitude for sparrows, surely He'll do something for His unfeathered friends?

I miss you a lot, Jeff, and especially so tonight. I have the curtains drawn and the candles lit and a fire in the fireplace. I'd give anything if you were stretched out on the sofa with a highball, a detective story, and a set of thoroughly rumpled hair. Janie has left Deborah with us overnight, while she and Bill are out having a little much-needed recreation. Deborah is sleeping in your bed, which has been barricaded with everything we could find short of paving stones and barbed wire. Every five minutes, however, I hear Father leave his room and tiptoe in to see that Deb-

22

orah hasn't fallen on the floor. I am more the phlegmatic type. I only go every seven minutes.

I'm too sleepy to finish this off with a series of well-rounded phrases. Let me know if there's anything you need. Could you send us a snapshot of yourself in uniform? We keep trying to imagine you, but it always turns out to look like General MacArthur.

Affectionately,
Gretchen

Dear Bro.,

Whee! (and other sounds indicative of pleasure).

In the ordinary way, nobody would have expected your letter to produce delight and gratification in the recipient. That suavely flowing prose of yours—I'm happy to see that barracks life hasn't altered it—doesn't conceal the fact that you've written me a perfect torrent of complaint, anger and outrage. And what I say is, Hallelujah! The dam has broken at last, and you've condescended to be aggrieved, self-pitying and—in other words—human. Tell me more. I love it.

It's too bad, Jeff, that you didn't open up like this a long time ago. But better late than never. I do think, though, that you're having a delayed reaction to Ellen's death, rather than a present reaction to Army life. You've got your signals mixed. Ellen's being killed was a shocking and hideously not-to-be-expected tragedy, and you certainly had the right to feel that

23

you had been singled out for misfortune. But there are quite a few other men who are being systematically annoyed by intrusive agencies like the Army . . .

I guess what I really liked about your letter is that it sets me free to talk about my brother Jeff—a subject you haven't, for some time, encouraged me to discuss. Jeff, why do you keep your eyes turned backward, like Lot's self-willed helpmate, to civilian life? Let's not kid ourselves about it. After Ellen was killed, your civilian life was an orderly arrangement of grief, loneliness and overwork. But looking back at it from Fort Bragg, you've begun to think of it as something jointly put together by Madame Curie and the Great God Pan. It wasn't really that way at all. It was pretty terrible, as a matter of fact.

I can imagine that the lack of privacy in your present environment is a severe trial, but don't forget that if the other soldiers intrude upon your solitude, you also intrude upon theirs. You'll say I'm looking at it with the serenity of somebody who doesn't have to face it, but I just can't believe, pet, that of the fifty men who share your boudoir, you are absolutely the only one with a taste for seclusion. Actually, the ones who have my sympathy are the unhappy warriors who have to sleep to the right and left of you. Handsome your teeth undoubtedly are, Skipper, but you grind them in your sleep. Your comrades in arms probably wish you had the kind that stands Retreat at night.

You suppose, you say, that the clumsy overtures of the other men are meant to be friendly, but you just

24

don't want to talk about yourself to every Tom, Dick and Harry. Aren't you being hypersensitive, Jeffie? They don't want to know anything about you that you don't want to tell them, but they have to find out what sort of person you are. They have to live with you. Perhaps they have to be under fire with you. Maybe all of them haven't got your Chesterfieldian polish, but their instinct, in this case, is sounder than yours.

I'm carrying on like the town scold, but it's only because I feel so helpless when I think of your unhappiness. Oh, darling, couldn't you sort of surge around and look for a fresh perspective? The one you have now would bring out goose-pimples on a morgue orderly. In the meantime, if it helps to blow off steam, why I am an old steam-lover from way back . . .

I have to stop now and get over to the Canteen. It's my night for handing out trays to the food line, a job which is generally considered enviable because you can sit down. Most of the hostesses' feet, at the Canteen, are in a state which would have provoked comment on the Retreat from Moscow (either one). The tray job really is easier, except for the fact that with every tray, you are supposed also to bestow a flashing smile. It's all right in the beginning, because I really like servicemen and it's no trouble to smile at them. But the shift is two and a half hours long, and the food line never stops. By the time I'm through, my sunny grin has turned into a sort of tic over which I have no control. As a matter of fact, I've nearly gotten into trouble a couple of times by beaming at the streetcar passengers on the way home, and even when I've reached my nice, quiet bedroom, I have to read a couple of chapters of *Mein Kampf* before I can sober off.

That's all for now, except to say once again that I was, paradoxically, delighted with your letter. Don't be angry with me for scolding you, and do try to remember, lambie-pie, that you don't have to close your pores every time anybody says hello.

Your loyal little "fan,"

Gretchen

January 20th

Dear Jeff,

I hope I'm really as busy as I think I am. I hope this hurried sensation doesn't just mean change of life. I'm going to collect a few bits and pieces for you every day, and mail it all at the end of the week, because I have to write a long memorandum to my Junior Hostesses and make fifty copies of it. The other captains have meetings, instead of writing to their girls, but the objection to that is you can never get more than half your hostesses to converge upon a given point at a given time. This leaves the other half free to say, whenever they break a rule, "Oh, but you never told me!"—a prerogative they exercise up to the hilt.

I love my Junior Hostesses—except for one or two condescending young chits who would be noticeably improved by a short sojourn in a meat grinder—but I am continually amazed at their inability to learn anything. They aren't supposed, for instance, to stand on the chairs and tables to see the entertainment. The Canteen furniture had lived a full life before it ever reached the Canteen, and it hasn't been eating its head off in the stable since we got it. Standing on it is the royal road to a compound fracture. All this I have explained to my babies, not once, but twenty times, yet a roll of dust can't blow across the stage without half a dozen Junior Hostesses scrambling up on the furniture to command a better view of it. What do you imagine goes on in their funny little minds? For myself, I no longer believe that Nature abhors a vacuum. I could show you some vacuums Nature is simply crazy about.

January 21st

Well, Jeffie dear,

We've finally rented your room—to a stockily built citizen named Tom Garrett, who flies Army freight and passengers to Scotland and Africa for one of the air lines. He wears a sort of Air Corps uniform, but only when he's flying. My seismograph puts him at about thirty-five. He's going to be here for a week or two at a time, and then be away for a while. This will give us intervals of privacy we'll be extremely grateful for, but it will also mean I'll have to get a new permanent. I can't pin up my hair while doing the housework if there's a sharp-eyed birdman streaming in and out. I hate getting a new permanent, because for the first week afterwards my hair always looks like a bowl of Rice Crispies, but with Mr. Garrett supplementing our income, I'll at least be able to afford it—an experience which will be distinctly novel.

I'd been worrying a good deal about how Father would behave toward the new tenant. Father is so deeply resentful of the necessity for having someone in the house, and so unwilling to assume any more airs and graces than pertain to the average crowbar, that I was afraid he would make the place uninhabitable for the stranger within our gates. But apparently he likes Mr. Garrett. When I came home from the Canteen last night, the two of them were drinking beer in the living room and talking like old cronies. Unreasonably enough, I was annoyed. I'd been all braced to protect the wayfarer against Father's curved talons and long yellow fangs, and then what does Popsy do but rub up against him and purr?

As a matter of fact, this Mr. Garrett needs protection about as much as I need a third breast. He isn't aggressive, but he isn't the least bit shy. Except for saying that he has all the qualities you are supposed to get from taking vitamin pills, I don't know how to describe his manner. His looks are easier. Though not tall, he is the owner of many plain and fancy muscles and they seem to be arranged upon his skeleton in a distinctly tasteful way. He has a very straight nose and beautiful brown eyes, but his face is too wide in the jaw and his hair, although dark and curly, is some day going to reach a point where it won't have a quorum.

I sound a little ungracious about him, don't I? I guess I resent his occupying my darling brother's room and bursting into our quiet house with his unwelcome vitality. But we advertised for him, and I must try to be fair—though it is not a field in which I have ever distinguished myself. He does make me realize keenly the extent to which I miss you.

January 22nd

What does little Jeffie say,
In his nest at break of day?

I haven't heard from you, and I'm afraid you're angry at my last letter. That couldn't be, could it, when I'm the apple of your eye and all?

January 23rd

I hope that many; many blessings, comforts, delights and gratifications were the reward of whoever designed the big casement window in our living room. It's snowing hard, and the window, with the bare tree beyond, is something I wish you could see, brother dear. (By squinting slightly, it's possible to shut out the garage wall which completes the vista.) I have lit the fire, which was extravagant of me, because logs are so expensive. But I had to be able to add, when telling you about the snow, that there is a fire burning

29

in the fireplace, as well as in the mirrors of the corner cabinets across the room, or otherwise you might not have felt cozy, might you?

I'll just round up the most recent bits of news, and then mail you the whole collection of the last four days when I go out to the Canteen tonight. I had lunch at Janie's yesterday, and am happy to report that Deborah now trots around with almost casual expertness and is growing to look considerably less top-heavy. She had her lunch in the kitchen—in her high chair— before we had ours, and Janie let me feed her. She's such a darling, Jeff! She sits and holds her mouth open like a fledgling bird, trustingly waiting for you to put food into it. But the feeding process, though terrifically engaging, is a speck on the gross side. Deborah doesn't know yet that all you need to eat with is your mouth. She's under the impression that it requires the entire face, and after three spoonfuls, she looks as if she'd fallen into the hands of a camouflage artist.

You'd be horrified if you could see the sort of stuff they give her to eat. It looks like a kind of beautifully processed garbage. Into fluid spinach, or carrots which have apparently tangled badly with an atom-smasher, the young mother puts various dark and ominous secretions deriving from liver. When this Lucullan mixture has been disposed of, the meal ends orgiastically with junket or trampled bananas. At the moment, Deborah doesn't appear to mind, but one day she's going to realize what we've been making her eat, and she'll probably move to the Y.W.C.A.

While Janie and I had lunch, Deborah circled tirelessly around the table, begging for crumbs. I myself had just fed her till the profile of her stomach could have held its own at a directors' meeting. But when she smiles up at me with her silly little amateur teeth and says hopefully, "Cooky?"—her generic term for anything to eat—I have a well-defined impulse to give her lobster à la Newburg and planked steak.

By the way, I am sending you some cookies. You ought to find them especially fortifying, because I cut my finger while chopping the nuts and the cookies are practically a blood transfusion in themselves. They may, in fact, have fought their way out of the box before they reach you. Mr. Tom Garrett came in while I was conducting my homemade shambles and bandaged my finger so tightly that I thought it was going to secede from the rest of me. The bandage did, however, stop the bleeding.

Our lodger then lit a cigarette (dropping the match on the floor) and sat on the kitchen stool talking while I finished putting the cooky batter together. I had to concentrate on the cookies, so I couldn't give him my full attention, but I was conscious that he was making up his mind what he thought about me, and it made me nervous. When he got up to go, I held up my bandaged finger and said, "Thank you, Mr. Garrett."

I was self-conscious, and my voice had all the wavering elegance of a barmaid at a vicarage tea. Mr. Garrett gave me what is known in the women's

31

magazines as a crooked smile, and said, "Call me Tom. Let's not be shabby-genteel."

Then he went down the hall, got into his coat, and went out.

Oh, Jeff, I can't *bear* it! A perfect stranger, and a rather rough-hewn one at that, comes into our house and puts his finger exactly on what has been worrying me ever since Pearl Harbor. I spend part of my time working at the Canteen, although I know it's a whited sepulcher. With the rest, I try to keep an apartment we can't afford cleaner than it can possibly be kept without a maid. When my grandchildren gather at my knee and ask me what I did to help win World War II, I shall have to answer, "Why, darlings, I took in boarders."

I tell myself that Father isn't a young man any more, and he needs this apartment to live in if he's going to do his job well. But if I worked in a war plant, I'd be doing more for my country than I do now, and I'd be bringing in money besides. You and Father would both survive the breaking up of our home. After all, lots of English people have had their home life arbitrarily rearranged by high explosive, and who are we, to be so self-indulgently clannish?

At this point in my one-man debate, I try to picture Father, uprooted, spending his evenings in a hotel room, and then I stop thinking altogether and just subside into an agony of indecision. Sometimes it seems to me people can bear absolutely anything, provided they don't have to make up their minds about it.

Just the same, I do not think Mr. Garrett and I would ever have had that rapport so conspicuously enjoyed by the Bobbsey Twins, even if he hadn't begun the acquaintance by treading heavily upon my spiritual corns. I can't honestly say he's bumptious, because he isn't, but he's definitely not the lad with the delicate air. And as for calling him by his first name—any time you hear me doing that, you can mount pom-pom guns on my larynx and send it out to sea.

Love,
Gretchen

January 27th

Jeffie dear,

That was an awfully sweet letter, and it was the more valuable and heartening because you sent it air mail special delivery. I was startled by your saying that Mr. Garrett sounds to you like a younger and more modern version of Father. If it's so, it gives me a nice, fat, sun-ripened grievance. No woman should be expected to live in the same house with *two* men like Father. You're in the Field Artillery, my friend. Let me know if you hear of a desirable barrage I could move into.

I'm flattered by your theory that Mr. Garrett was trying to attract my attention with his somewhat startling remark, but I don't think I want a boy just like the boy that married Dear Old Mother. I would, in fact, quarrel with your sweet reasonableness about Mr. Garrett, if I weren't so enamored of your sweet reasonableness about me. Those were lovely things you said about me, Jeff, and I'm going to have the phrase about my being loyal and sturdily patient tattooed on my back. It will certainly dazzle the Emergency Ward interns, if I ever get the falling sickness.

I accept as right—pray Heaven not because it is so convenient!—your statement that Father could survive the house being wrecked by a bomb, because it would be an Act of God, but that he's not flexible enough any more to accept its being wrecked by an Act of Gretchen.

With a view to prejudicing you a little against Mr. Garrett, I mention in passing that he is a slob of the first magnitude. The first few days, he made a short-lived and halfhearted effort to keep your room neat, but he has now openly abandoned the unnatural effort. By working ten hours a day, I manage to keep his chamber almost up to the standards maintained by a self-respecting abattoir.

But that's enough of griping. It was a wonderful letter, Jeff, and I can't tell you how much it did for me.

Gratefully,
Me Too

Brother Dear:

There's never any use getting angry with a Southerner on account of what he says about Negroes, because no matter how angry you get, he can always raise you five. As a piece of advice, this dictum is not the low-powered affair it seems at first glance, but I'll get to that in a minute. Your exchange of hostilities with the Southern sergeant gave me, I must admit, a moment of not wholly charitable pleasure. Maybe it's been unconscious—I guess it has—but both you and Father have always been rather patronizing about my working at the Canteen, dismissing it as some sort of sentimental, womanish frippery I had got myself into that was harmless but not important. I'm the first to concede that a serviceman can't have as much fun at the Columbus Circle Canteen as he could by taking a suite in a hotel and having double Scotches and beautiful, compliant women sent up every fifteen minutes. But the Canteen is the only organization of its kind in the country that has never discriminated against Negroes, either as servicemen or as civilian workers. Since it doesn't discriminate against Southerners, either, I too have had my baptism of ire.

If I break it to you gently, may I tell you that the sergeant won the dispute? You fell into a trap, Jeffie. I speak with the melancholy wisdom of one who has fallen into it many, many times herself.

Here's how it is.

35

What, in essence, did you want to do? You wanted to shake the sergeant's faith in a legend he's partial to about the natural inferiority of Negroes to white people. The sergeant didn't want you to shake that faith, and he kept you from doing it. He baited you with stories about what he had done to Negroes in the past and what he was going to do to Negroes in the future, and you got angry and horrified and told him—fluently, if I know my Jeffie—that he was cruel. But the sad fact is, Jeff, that he doesn't give a tinker's curse whether you think he's cruel, so long as he can go on believing.

Suppose you hadn't taken the bait. Suppose you'd stayed calm and said equably, "All right, I'm a professional scientist and as such, I hope, a not unreasonable man. I'll accept your theory of the natural inferiority of Negroes, if you'll prove it to me. I don't mean prove it by something your Aunt Nellie's houseboy said in 1916. I mean prove it the way I'm used to having things proved—with statistics and figures and experiments."

The sergeant, like all Americans, has been taught to revere science. The one thing he doesn't want to have called to his attention is what science says about the myth of race. You could have put the burden of proof on the sergeant, but he outmaneuvered you. You not only didn't shake his faith in his inexact legend, but you encouraged him to think that the same tactics will work with the next Northerner who tries to set him right. Which they probably will.

36

I hope you don't think I'm unsympathetic, darling. I'm not. I know how baffled and heartsick you felt, because I've been through it myself. When I first went to the Canteen—never having been South or met any Southerners—I lapped up a quantity of shock treatment after listening to some of the Southern servicemen talk about the Negroes. You can't do your shopping near Third Avenue without once in a while hearing what a truck driver says to a drunk who almost falls under his wheels, but never in my life had anybody spoken to me personally and at length about sex and assault and rape and hitting people and burning people over slow fires. What got me thoroughly confused was that the Southern boys claim this sort of talk gets away big with Southern womanhood and makes them feel pure. Out of Northern womanhood, it scares the well-known bejesus.

I was new at the Canteen then, and I didn't know some of the people there as well as I do now. You and Ellen were in California, and you can imagine how much help Father would have been. So I had to work it out myself, and I began to realize, after a while—possibly just in self-defense—that these Southerners didn't *ask* to be brought up feeling the way they do about Negroes. They didn't look up from their bassinets and say, "Mother, please teach me a legend about Negroes that is going to make me nervous, the Negroes wretched, and people on other continents kind of sick." The reason we Northerners are so appalled when we hear Southerners discussing race is that we assume the Southerners embraced race prejudice deliberately, when they had their choice of not doing so. But they didn't have any choice. Not, at least, when they were little.

I've come to believe, from working at the Canteen, that we in the North are a good deal too smug about our freedom (such as it is) from race prejudice. We point to it with pride, as if it were some special kind of native virtue on our part, whereas in reality it's only a geographical accident. If we'd been born in the South and brought up as the current generations of living Southerners were brought up, we'd be exactly the way they are. The uncomfortable truth, Jeff, is that the North uses the Southerners as an excuse for not doing anything about the race problem itself. We read the Southerners pious, condescending lectures about lynching, but a Negro—no matter how well bred, well dressed and well educated—can't rent an apartment in New York outside of Harlem. Nor can he buy a dinner and stay overnight at a midtown hotel. The North permits Negroes to vote, and to sit anywhere they want in a streetcar. But how much of one's time does one generally spend voting? And while a streetcar is a perfectly acceptable public utility, it's no place to bring up the children.

By the most uncritical standards, Harlem is not an earthly paradise. The Harlem Hospital was understaffed and brutally overcrowded long before we were at war. The cost of food and shelter in Harlem is way above what it is for comparable commodities in other parts of the city. When you consider that we aren't handicapped by the Southerner's intensive and practically intra-uterine education about the Negro's "place," the moral eminence from which we look down on the South is nothing to make anybody giddy. Feeling the way they do about Negroes, the Southerners are naturally not going to urge us to establish racial democracy in the North or anywhere else; but they haven't failed to note that we don't practice what we preach, and I think it's one reason why we make so little headway when we try to argue with them.

I'm getting quite a bounce out of writing this letter, Bro.—race relations being the only field outside of housekeeping where I've accumulated a little bit of personal, practical experience. Also, I shan't outlive my gratitude that you conducted most of my education practically singlehanded, whereas the only thing I was ever in a position to teach you was how to distinguish, at thirty paces and with both hands tied behind you, whether a young lady is wearing a girdle. It took you such a short time to learn, too!

Anyway, I used to think, before I went to the Canteen, that the only way to solve the race problem was the hard way. I used to think that if you couldn't establish racial equality overnight in Mississippi and Alabama, there was nothing to do but sit back and wait for the ensuing carnage. But now I've begun to believe that the way to tackle the race problem is the easy way. You can't do much about prejudice in the South, but you can do quite a lot about lethargy in

39

the North. In this highly mobile age, ideas and practices travel fast; but they can't travel at all unless they have a home base *somewhere*. Why does it have to be in Mississippi?

About six or eight per cent of the servicemen we entertain at the Canteen are Negroes, and among my personal collection of Junior Hostesses, I have five Negro girls. Very nice girls they are, too. All of them are either college students or college graduates, which is more than can be said for their captain. After I found out how many places those girls can't go and how many things they can't do, right here in New York, I stopped worrying about the South. Just this morning I learned that some patriotic organization— I haven't found out which one, but I will—asked for some of our Junior Hostesses to collect funds in places of public assemblage; but they sent back a Negro girl who volunteered, though she is a light-skinned and personable creature.

"We don't want Negroes," was their somewhat boorish way of expressing it to her.

It might well be that the citizenry, confronted by a pretty young Negress soliciting money for a worthy cause, would clutch its pocketbook to its heart and run screaming in the opposite direction. But how did this outfit know? They hadn't tried.

I wish I had more time to go into this, but I'm only writing at all because you're making such heavy weather of things right now and your sister Gretchen is yearning over you. This yearning is taking place at the expense of my cloudy mirrors and dusty lamp shades, and is therefore to be regarded as a very high type emotion. Anyway, don't take on about the sergeant, Jeffie. Pay him no mind. I talk till my throat is hoarse with Southerners who are disposed to be polite about the race question, but when they carry on like the sergeant, I have learned to say, "The back of my hand to you, sir," and walk off. After all, they aren't forced to come into the Canteen in the first place, and they aren't forced to stay there if they don't like it; and if they start laying about them, the M.P.'s take them away.

Darling, don't agonize about the South. You won't be there very long, and the thing to think about is what you're going to do when the war is over and you're back in the North. I know one thing you can do. The next time you take on an assistant at the lab, you can employ a Negro, if a qualified one is available. Does that startle you? It would have startled me once, but not being startled by it is very good fun. Why beat your head against a wall? The sergeant is hopeless, but you've got better than a fighting chance to educate Miss Ellsworth and Friends.

Yours in haste, my poor, sad brother—

Gretchen

Dear Jeff,

Do you know what I'm up against? Helen Hokinson's Law—i.e., that there is an inverse ratio between a woman's mammary development and the power of her mind. What brought me to this esoteric subject is Mrs. Richards, who provides ballast—if she does nothing else—on the Canteen's Governing Board. Mrs. Richards has a bosom mature enough to have nourished a couple of mastodons, but intellectually she couldn't hold her own with Little Eva.

I went to the Canteen office yesterday to see her, and found her telephoning the U. S. O. on behalf of a shy young soldier who was standing next to her desk. All of a sudden, in the middle of a sentence, she said, "Oh, I forgot the linoleum company!" and hung up the phone. While the soldier and I gaped, she began going through the desk drawers like a delirious terrier. At this interesting juncture, somebody stopped in the doorway and said there was a public relations man downstairs. Mrs. Richards paused just long enough to clasp her hands and moan, "Oh, I have so much *work* to do!" Then she got away from the desk like a racehorse spurning the barrier and skittered off downstairs.

My own idea is that it's a pitiable waste to keep all the women like Mrs. Richards cooped up on the home front. I think we should ship them to Europe with the invasion troops and send them in ahead of the tanks. A Prussian general is conditioned to mortar fire and thinks of land mines as being all in the day's work; but five minutes of conversation with Mrs. Richards, and he'd hand her his sword and take the first rocket to Mars.

Mrs. Richards and her husband and Mrs. Alicia Sadler are the only people on the Governing Board who ever come to the Canteen. Mr. Richards is a tall man with what must have been a magnificent build before his stomach went in for a career of its own. Having mentioned that, I discover it is absolutely the only halfway favorable thing I can find to say about him. Unless it is favorable to say that he differs from Mrs. Alicia Sadler in being a passive sourpuss, whereas she is an active one. If you can imagine Ivan the Terrible at the moment of discovering he has lost a filling, that gives you an idea of Mr. Richards' customary expression. Fortunately, he talks little. His manner, when he does speak, is so disagreeable and autocratic that most people would rather spend the evening with a process server than say hello to Mr. R. Except when the periscope officer reports news photographers on the horizon, Mr. Richards never does any work at the Canteen. He just drops in and stands around startling people with his resemblance to the Grim Reaper.

Do you find all this stuff about the Canteen tedious, Jeffie? If so, you have only to nudge me and I'll shut up. But you were in California when I was first getting the hang of the place, and I never did have much chance to talk to you about it. Not that I've entirely gotten the hang of it even yet. The Governing Board, for instance, is a sort of legend to the people who work at the Canteen. Except for Mrs. Sadler and the Richardses, we never see them in person, but we see their pictures in the papers, with aprons on and an admiring caption underneath stating that they faithfully serve coffee to the darling, darling soldiers umpteen nights a week. These pictures are supposed to be for "morale," but the legend doesn't specify whose. They certainly don't improve the morale of the ladies who whirl in from Brooklyn and Washington Heights in their monogrammed, velvet-lined subway coaches and really *do* serve the coffee. The servicemen, too, always seem mildly surprised to find the coffee administered by exactly the same sort of women from whom they have been receiving coffee all their lives. Not that they appear to mind—in fact, I think it comforts them—but from newspapers, radio broadcasts and magazines they have gotten the impression that when they came to the Canteen, they would find the entire Governing Board (a very classy aggregation of name and fame) folding paper napkins for them. This expectation, though entirely false and unable to survive the cold touch of reality, is known as "morale."

"Morale" came close to home one night last week, when I turned on the radio and heard Millie Calvert speaking. Miss Calvert is on the Governing Board at the Canteen, and though I know you don't like her books, I think myself that in some ways she's even better than Jane Austen and thoroughly deserves her success. On the radio, Miss Calvert was recounting how, when she had left the Canteen the previous evening, she encountered a tired and resentful Junior Hostess who was just about to give the whole thing up. Miss Calvert's story of the way in which she talked the Junior Hostess into continuing was moving and effective. Whatever you say, Jeff, Millie Calvert writes like an angel, and she had the vox humana stop pulled all the way out. I would, quite literally, have had a lump in my throat, if I hadn't known that it's a year and two months since Miss Calvert has set foot in the Canteen, and on that occasion she was surrounded by enough secretaries, press agents and photographers to staff the Throne of God. Any Junior Hostess even wanting to shake hands with her would have had first to clear the path with a portable death ray. Some of my own hostesses happened to hear Miss Calvert and they were much amused. Their merriment, in fact, was of the kind generally attributed to horses.

Since the members of the Governing Board have the mythical quality of absentee landlords, it's hard for a Canteen worker to decide what they are really like. Presumably they are fairly amiable people, and certainly they raise money for the Canteen. Nor can they be held responsible for the fact that newspapers would rather have an artificial story with a name than a real one with inconspicuous people. But all we who really work there know about the Board is what we can figure out from the fact that some of its members accept lavish publicity for things they don't do—a situation that cannot be ascribed entirely to absentmindedness. So far as the civilians are concerned, it doesn't matter; but it makes one a little nervous to feel that we're systematically misleading the servicemen.

When I was in high school, Skipper, and you were supervising my English themes, you were relentless on the subject of graceful transitions. But you just tell me, Maestro, how I get from the Governing Board to Tom Garrett by any process less definitive than a pole vault. He's been away for a week—our lodger, I mean. The last night he was here, he came in about eleven o'clock and handed me a bottle of Scotch. I was so taken aback I just stood there, holding the Scotch, and said accusingly, "You think I'm shabby-genteel."

He laughed and said, "You didn't like that? I'm sorry, but I never can resist the temptation to make a sow's ear out of a silk purse."

"You mean me?" I asked stupidly. One of the least agreeable things about him is that he always makes me feel as if I had adenoids right down to my navel.

"Little short of," he said.

I swallowed, which was a bad idea, because it turned out I didn't have enough saliva, and asked him if he'd have a drink.

He agreed with what I believe is known as alacrity, so we fixed drinks. It was late and the house was very quiet. I had asked Father if he would help me balance my checkbook, but he said, "Character is destiny," and went to bed. There was hail plucking fretfully at the windows, and the fire had burned down to a big bed

46

of embers. I had cleaned closets all day, and was full of the ineffable superiority that comes from knowing our Hallowe'en costumes, Scout knives and old diplomas are dusted and ready for instant use. As we sat down in the living room, it occurred to me that I could get the upper hand of our lodger by leading him to talk about himself, instead of me—a policy no woman would describe as uphill work.

The only trouble with this idea was that he saw through it at once, and in virtually nothing flat we were discussing, not Mr. Garrett, but the undersigned. In the ordinary way, this would have delighted me, as there is no subject I feel is more replete with interesting and attractive surprises. But in the hands of Mr. Tom Garrett, the surprises are less of the Christmas-stocking kind and more like finding a centipede in your shoe. He said I lived too sheltered a life—just staying at home basking in the admiration of my father and brother and letting life pass me by. Do you see what I mean, Jeff? I'm supposed to be the one who says I'm letting life pass me by, and Mr. Tom Garrett is supposed to say No, no, a thousand times no. From then on, we would be great friends. But how can I be friends with somebody who takes all my lines in the dialogue?

It's bad enough not to get to sleep at night from thinking that time is passing and I'm not doing anything with myself. But it's simply unbearable to hear it before bedtime from somebody I don't even know very well. I got so nervous, at the turn the conversa-

47

tion took, that I had another drink—spurred by which, I told him about Philip and the manifold inconveniences (to mince a word) of having been married to same. I confess, though I wouldn't admit it to anybody but you, that I expected a strongly sympathetic reaction, interlarded with murmurs of "Poor Butterfly!" and similar fortifying sentiments. But although he was interested and asked a lot of questions, the Poor Butterfly angle didn't seem to occur to him. Feeling rather like a puppy whose decomposed rabbit has failed to please the folks at home, I switched the conversation to the Canteen. Here I hit the jack pot. Mr. Tom Garrett thinks the Canteen is wonderful. The phony publicity which has been making me so uneasy he says is laughable but not important. What kindled his by no means halfhearted enthusiasm was the no-discrimination policy. He himself got introduced to the race problem somewhat abruptly, having once been pulled out of a crashed plane by a Negro newspaperman when the other bystanders were entertaining justifiable apprehensions about the gas tanks exploding. Mr. G. used to see quite a lot of his rescuer before he—the Negro—went into the Army.

Warmed by the first sign of approval I've ever seen in our paying guest, I expanded about the Canteen. If you could have seen how much interested he was, Jeffie darling, you'd be sorry you ever thought of it as a debutante enterprise (she threatened). Mr. Tom Garrett says it's the most forward-looking place he ever heard of, because it gives white people the opportunity to meet a diversity of Negroes. What has it been like?—he wanted to know. This gave me pause, because I've never stopped to review it. In the beginning, it certainly involves a slight adjustment. When you first work on committees with Negroes and meet them socially, you're terribly conscious of the dark skin and highly embarrassed for fear they'll know you're conscious of it. But that wears off quickly, and you learn to think of them just as assorted people, without reference to their pigmentation.

Thinking of them just as people has to be learned. In the first flush of your enthusiasm, you tend to regard them as the Wonderful Oppressed; and it comes as an anti-climax to find that they can be just as disagreeable or narrow-minded or boring as citizens who have never been put upon. I don't know why one should make the assumption that being oppressed automatically creates a flawless character, but almost everybody at the Canteen did make it, at the start. A few people didn't survive it, and they went away from there.

Once past the Wonderful Oppressed stage, you're in the clear—at least, as far as you yourself are concerned. There are still your fifty Junior Hostesses, about two-thirds of whom wouldn't mind being unprejudiced about Negroes if they could get over being afraid of them. (The other third was unprejudiced in the first place.) Looking back on it, the main thing that stands out in my mind is how much time we all wasted trying to dazzle the Junior Hostesses with theories, while we ignored what was really on their minds. I spent hours and hours talking to my girls about democracy and the Constitution, and then discovered inadvertently one day that what preoccupies many of them is the idea that Negroes have a different body odor from ours. So I put the Constitution away in moth balls, and nowadays I start right in by saying that a sweat gland is a sweat gland, and since Negroes have the same kind we have, they couldn't possibly smell any different. No overheated serviceman suggests trailing arbutus, but nobody could pass a blindfold test on what color he is.

By dint of comparing notes over a long period of time, a lot of the captains found out that if you don't immobilize the girls with talk of ethics and democracy, there are always two questions they finally get around to asking. The first is, "What about intermarriage?" I found a gray hair the other day, Jeff—at twenty-six—and I ascribe it entirely to the weedlike prevalence of the belief that Negro men want nothing so much in the world as to marry white women. If this is true, the darker brother has certainly been overlooking a golden opportunity at the Canteen, because so far as we know, no Negro boy has ever asked a Caucasian girl for her hand in marriage—or if one has, she hasn't mentioned it. This always surprises people who have had no experience of servicemen, but veteran civilians know that the armed forces don't drop into a canteen with the idea of popping the question to the first reasonably symmetrical female they see. Most of them have wives or sweethearts back home. (At least, they hope they still have.) You discover this when you talk to them, and find you can pass as a brilliant conversationalist with only two sentences—the first sentence being, "Gosh!" and the second, "And what did she do when you said *that?*"

At any rate, when my girls pluck up their courage and ask shyly about intermarriage, I tell them that they are not likely to have the chance to marry a Negro; and if they do have, and he is not the moon of their delight that knows no wane, they can always say no. Many uncomplimentary things have been said about the institution of marriage (some of them by me), but even its strongest detractors don't claim that it's compulsory.

The second question the Junior Hostesses ask is, "Suppose I fall in love with one?"

I once heard a girl put this query to one of our top-notch Senior Hostesses. (The Senior Hostesses are not usually held in esteem by the Juniors, who find them autocratic and refer to them as the Prairie Schooners, but a few of them are universally beloved and transcend even the critical faculties of the Junior Hostesses.)

"Suppose you fall in love with a Negro?"

The Senior Hostess shrugged lightly.

"Suppose you fall in love with a soldier who's already married. See that you don't, that's all."

"If you're so susceptible," she added whimsically, "that you fall in love while dancing twice around the

51

room with a total stranger, you ought not to be working in a canteen at all."

By this time, the girl who had raised the question was looking as if she were sorry she had brought it up, and the older woman noticed and put a reassuring arm around her.

"When you meet a Negro soldier," she said kindly, "you know right away that he *is* a Negro, whereas a married soldier might omit to mention the fact."

This letter, pet, must be well beyond the point of diminishing returns. But it's not my fault. It's the typewriter. I've just cleaned the type, and I can't do a thing with it. Anyway, Mr. Tom Garrett can be very imaginatively sympathetic when he forgets about carrying that banner with "Excelsior!" on it. I was so pleased with him for applauding the Canteen and dismissing my apprehensions about the publicity, that when a suitable cadence arose, I managed to call him by his first name. It came out with all the happy spontaneity of a Caesarean section, but I felt I owed it to him.

When we exchanged good nights, I said it was nice of him to wrestle with the Lord for my soul, but I wished it didn't involve his being so frequently rude.

"I'm rude," he said, "because too many men are polite to you. It isn't good for you."

"Philip wasn't polite to me," I snapped, and instantly regretted my childishness.

He made a derogatory grimace.

"Anybody can be rude when he's drunk all the time.

52

But I can be rude to you when I'm cold sober."

"It seems a peculiar accomplishment."

"But an accomplishment," he said. "Good night."

And I'll have to say good night, too, Jeff. It's so late I'm going to wind the clock without looking at it, so I won't know in the morning how little sleep I've had.

Affectionately,

Gretchen

February 5th

Jeffie dear,

I started to write to you yesterday, but the plumber came to fix the hot water faucet which has had auto-intoxication since shortly after you left for the Army. We've got a new faucet now, and although it doesn't match the other and is labeled "Cold" instead of "Hot," at least we don't have to wash our hands and faces over the bathtub any more. Of course, both faucets are now marked "Cold," and when Bonnie McKay—one of the other Junior Hostess captains— stopped in yesterday and was subsequently ushered into the bathroom, she looked at the basin and said, "I heard you the first time."

Aside from the new faucet, there isn't any particular news. Father and I are having one of our spells of being irritated with each other. Father wouldn't help me balance the checkbook, so I had to do it the best

I could myself. I balanced it, but when Father found the document on my worktable, he was seriously displeased because the last line read:

$18.91 the bank took which doesn't belong to it.

Father intimated that as the fruit of his loins, I was very small potatoes, especially on the intellectual side. I maintained with some heat that if it comes out even at the bottom, it's balanced; but this soothing and reasonable concept operated on Popsy like a burr under the saddle.

"You've got to account for the $18.91," he kept saying angrily.

"I *have* accounted for it. The bank took it. They're trying to make ends meet."

It ended with my going out to a newsreel and Father, I suspect, calling up the bank to apologize for what I'd said about them.

February 6th

I didn't finish my letter yesterday, because I had an intuition there'd be one from you this morning, and my prophetic bones turned out to be in perfect working condition. Your letter was very bitter, darling, but I have dug my toes in and I refuse to accept your unflattering version of yourself. You dwell with emphasis, to say the least, upon your inferior physique and upon the fact that you're a misfit in the Army. As far as your physique is concerned, I grant you that in a bathing suit you look as if you'd just been taken down from the Cross. But I can't help remembering that not so very long ago you were playing a superior game of tennis—in your own sparse flesh, too, and not with the aid of photo-electric cells.

As for being a misfit, pooh! In a civilian draft Army, you can't fire BB shot into an advancing platoon without hitting a misfit. All the guys who were influenced by sunspots to be military men were in the Army before we ever thought of having to go to war. The rest are all misfits, in the sense that they'd much rather be doing something else, but they happen to be the only thing we've got with which to win the war. We always fight the Germans with misfits—remember?—and after we've won, they always say it was beginner's luck.

I've got my own theory about adjustment to Army life. I mean, adjustment by the older and very definitely not military men like you. I think it has three stages. The first is post-operative shock, the result of having the carefully built up personal identity taken away and an insultingly astronomical serial number substituted instead. The second stage is very intense self-preoccupation, similar to what you find in certain phases of t.b. I think this is the stage you're in now. In the third stage, the Army begins to assert itself and the victims start to sit up, talk about their "outfits," and condescend to civilians.

As a civilian, I'm waiting eagerly for the day when you begin to patronize me, though when it comes I shall probably point out crisply that the home front isn't the bed of roses it used to be when it was just a home and not a front. Not that I'm complaining. On the contrary, I'm such a rip-roaring patriot that I even subscribe, in public, to the woman's page fantasy that meat loaf extended with soybeans cannot be distinguished from the peacetime version. Privately, I am free to admit that I've eaten the sawdust from too many dolls to be fooled for a minute by soybeans. I'm a loyal adherent of point rationing, too—that is to say, I'm loyal, but I don't know whether my inept thrashings-about could, strictly speaking, be described as adherence. You, whose lifelong affection for me barely survived some of the things I did in Intermediate Algebra, can imagine the welter I make of it. I get confused and add wrong, so the end of every week finds me trying to lay hands on a can of salmon with an assortment of points that wouldn't buy a culture for a germ.

It is my contention that one lobe of my brain is missing and I should be humored, but Father claims that I could understand rationing, or any other kind of figures, if I really wanted to.

"What," he asked me, "do you *think* about when you're milling around that kitchen?"

"Well," I said, "this morning, when I was cleaning the silver, I was thinking that I wished I could see a policeman crying, so I could say my cop runneth over."

Father didn't press the matter.

Anyway, Jeff, I don't think you're physically inferior and I don't think you're a misfit in the Army. I think you're essentially, as well as superficially, a wonderful gent, and I subscribe to the popular notion about when the darkest hour comes.

As to your crack about my having fallen in love with Tom Garrett, I think it comes more from the fact that you are suffering pain and anger and self-doubt than from any profound study of the situation. You'll have to do better than that to get a rise out of me, Jeff. I've been around this rancid apartment for so long, I could fall in love with Dracula. In fact, if you're right, I have. But you overlook the circumstance that your absence leaves a big hole in my life and Tom, though possessing all the entertainment value of a trip to the dentist, is at least someone to talk to after Father's gone to bed. Besides, the war has speeded up everybody's emotions—yours and mine and possibly even those stumpy little sensations which course through Mr. Tom Garrett.

But when you add it all up, it doesn't spell sweet-heart. For one thing, I'm not physically attracted to short, muscular men, even when they don't have jaws like a snowplow. For another thing, Tom Garrett's interest in me is purely therapeutic. It's less like the poet contemplating a tender windflower than like the surgeon yearning over an outsize hernia.

That's enough Shrewd Insight for one day, so I will close. I have mailed you a big package of magazines. I hope the pictures of *Life* going to an opium den will give you a momentary respite.

Love,

Gretchen

57

Dear Jeff,

I haven't written you because a week ago today Father had a heart attack. But don't worry. He's all right. He went back to the office this morning. What frightened me was more his state of mind than his state of body. He was desperately depressed. After he'd been in bed four days, I typed out a letter for him he'd written to Uncle John. It was full of bitter references to mistakes he'd made and ends he'd left untied, and the whole tone was one of raging regret and anguished self-contempt.

I was terribly startled, this being a side of him I'd never seen before. As a conversationalist, he has many points of resemblance to potassium cyanide, but I've always loved him for looking so much like Mark Twain and respected him because of his native capacity for being two jumps ahead of me. I don't think I ever told you—you were away for the summer at the time—but once when I was seventeen I decided to make an experiment in social relations by using the phrase "bawdy house" at breakfast one morning.

Father slapped the table so hard the oatmeal went up into stalagmites.

"Young girls," he thundered, "are supposed to call them bordellos."

That's the sort of thing that has kept my admiration for him alive, even through those not infrequent moments when I feel as if I'm keeping house for a Stanley

58

Steamer. After the first shock of having to re-focus, I began to feel painfully sorry for him. After all, people like you and me are accustomed to self-doubt, but to Father it must have all the hideous novelty of coming down with the black plague. I wanted to go in and, as Janie used to say, kiss it all better; but you know Father. He would have been embarrassed, and among the many varmints whose skins he nails to the barn door, people who embarrass him are well in the lead.

So I kept quiet and went out and mailed his letter. While I was out I bought a rose, which I put on his supper tray with a note saying, "Smile for the lady. Show the little toofies." I heard him laugh when he read the note, and when I went in to get the empty tray, he said in a pleased voice that I was just like my mother—which, as you know, is our fireside version of the Congressional Medal.

After that evening, he wasn't depressed any more and the next afternoon the doctor let him get up. To-day he wrote to Uncle John again—I imagine to say, "Excuse it, please." The doctor says in spite of his heart, he's exceptionally healthy for his age. He said he wished some of his other patients had Father's will to live. At any rate, the Progenitor seems much rested for his week at home, and if you are looking around for things to worry about, I think you'll have to con-sider the old man out of bounds.

I have to stop now. Our handsome but decaying domicile took the bit in its teeth while Father was sick,

59

and only a series of lunatic self-deceptions enables me to ignore the fact that we're now living on Tobacco Road.

Love,
Gretchen

February 16th

Gosh, Jeffie, am I in a state! Something happenea at the Canteen last night which, from the point of view of moral values, was pure essence of nux vomica. I have a girl on my shift named Mae Rabinowitz. She's an enthusiastic, instinctively friendly person, and while not exactly pretty, she owns and occupies some fine teeth and a pair of heart-softening dimples. Unfortunately, Mae has one noticeable shortcoming: When she gets excited, her voice rises to a pitch generally considered suitable only for hog-calling. I've spoken to her about it—assuming for the purpose an inflection which would have given Whistler's Mother a twinge of professional jealousy—and I know she does try to keep her voice down, but she's young (18) and sometimes she forgets.

Last night I was prowling around looking for timid souls who need their Junior Hostesses cut up for them, like a toddler's meat, when I found myself standing next to Mrs. Alicia Sadler. This is a location which I seek at all times to avoid, since I have seen many a dyspeptic cobra with whom I feel more at home than I do with Mrs. S. I had just given her the sickly, appeasing smile which I regret to say she brings out on me, and was about to drift away, when she shot out an arm and grabbed a merchant seaman by the shoulder. He was standing alone, a little ahead of her, and he turned a sullen face and eyed her coldly.

"Young man," said Mrs. Sadler autocratically, "get out on that floor and dance."

I don't know how to describe it, Jeff. We have other imperious old ladies around the Canteen, but they do not have the complete absence of solicitude for the servicemen which makes Mrs. Sadler's ministrations so exactly parallel to the Russian winter.

"I don't wanta dance," the seaman said, and shook off Mrs. Sadler's hand.

I won't say Mrs. Sadler's face hardened, because at best, a horse riding over it would certainly strike sparks. But her innate uncharity visibly deepened, and she reached for the seaman again.

"Go and dance," she commanded.

The seaman shrugged off the hand a second time.

"Are you deaf, lady? I told you I don't wanta dance."

He started to walk away, and then he turned back and smiled at her maliciously.

"I got hit, see," he said distinctly. "I can't dance no more."

There was a little gasp from the people standing around who had been watching the dance floor and unavoidably listening to this exchange. As the seaman disappeared into the crowd, it was apparent that he limped.

61

That was the moment I heard Mae. She was sitting at a table too far away to have witnessed the incident with the seaman, but she was audible for miles. There were three soldiers at the table with her, two of them very good-looking, and clearly she'd had quite a little success with them and it had intoxicated her. The soldiers were laughing noisily, too, and the whole table was not a thing you'd expect to find in a cloister.

Mrs. Sadler listened; then her lips curled with vindictive satisfaction and she started in the direction of Mae. I lit out after her, trying to get to Mae first, and as I said Excuse-me, excuse-me, excuse-me to the people I mangled in my progress, I saw Bonnie McKay bearing down on Mae from the opposite direction. I tried to catch Mae's eye and signal her behind Mrs. Sadler's back, but she was absorbed and didn't look at me. Mrs. Sadler swept up to her, took her wrist in a vicious grasp, and said furiously, "Will you *stop* that yelling?"

Mae broke off her sentence in the middle, and the soldiers stared, obviously trying to make head or tail of the contrast between Mrs. Sadler's saintly white hair and her conversational resemblance to a Mark IV tank. Bonnie opened her mouth to speak, and I started forward. But Mrs. Sadler looked first at Bonnie, then at me, and then at nobody at all.

"As soon as I can find the time," she said to the empty air, "I'm going to clean up this place and get rid of the Jews."

Then she put up one ringed hand, fluffed the lace at her throat, and pattered away.

After a long, long while, I realized that Bonnie and Mae and I, not to mention the soldiers, couldn't go on playing Still-Pond-No-More-Moving all night. Mae turned her head and the tears came to her eyes and started to run down her cheeks. Bonnie dragged up a chair and sat down at the table. I pulled Mae to her feet, asked the soldiers to excuse her, and took her to the cloakroom. As we walked away, I heard Bonnie saying, "Don't look now, but we've got a blot on our escutcheon," and one of the soldiers said in a small voice, "Wow!"

In the cloakroom, I pinned my captain's badge on the first girl I could find who looked moderately capable; borrowed fifty cents for taxi fare; and took Mae over to our house. She didn't say anything. She didn't even, technically, cry. It was just that the tears kept running down her cheeks. When we got home, I was surprised to find Tom Garrett lying on the sofa reading. He'd been away, and I hadn't expected him back so soon. Father, he said, had gone to his room to work, after first lighting the fire in the living room and suggesting that Tom would be more comfortable there than in his own room. If I hadn't been so upset about Mae, I would have been annoyed with Father, who expects me to keep the household accounts down to a figure he must have gotten from the Hopi Indians and then goes around setting fire to valuable, precious, expensive, New York City logs.

I introduced Mae and told Tom what had happened. It was Tom's idea that I should go and make Mae some cocoa, which I did. When I came back, Mae was sobbing into the sofa cushions and Tom was plying her with Kleenex and egging her on. She sat up when I brought the cocoa.

"We get used to this, you know," she said in a choked-up voice, "but I never thought it would happen at the Canteen. I thought that was one place . . . oh, it's so hopeless!"

"No, it isn't," Tom answered cheerfully. "Your friend Gretchen isn't going to take this lying down."

"Oh, yes, I am. I'm going to take it lying down so flat you could play billiards on me."

I gave Mae the cocoa.

Tom regarded me quizzically.

"Too proud to fight?"

"Let's be real," I said. "Mrs. Sadler is one of the founders of the Canteen and one of its heaviest contributors. Even Mrs. S. wouldn't have said what she did if she hadn't been snubbed to a fare-thee-well by a merchant seaman. But having said it, she isn't going to regret it for a moment, because there's nothing anybody can do to make her regret it."

Tom smiled.

"Isn't there? Arise-my-soul-stretch-all-thy-wings-and-press-with-vigor-on. I'm now going to take Miss Rabinowitz home, and if you'll wait up for me . . ."

Mae interrupted to say that he mustn't take her home, because she lived in Brooklyn. Tom answered that he'd just come back from Africa and he could spit to Brooklyn, at which Mae was sufficiently recovered to dimple faintly.

64

They left, and it was an hour and a half before Tom got back. The interval, Jeffie boy, is not one I look back on with retrospective pleasure. I took a warm bath, and drank some hot milk, and wound up with a cold shower, but none of these measures obscured the fact that I hate being in a fight and I was more than half hoping Tom wouldn't be able to think of anything to do. I could be caught dropping boulders on a sleeping kitten and have more sense of personal worth, but there it was.

When Tom came back, I started talking before he even got his coat off.

"This is how it will be. In three days the Junior Hostess captains have one of their regular meetings. Bonnie McKay and I will tell what happened tonight. The captains will be in an uproar, but what can they do? Mrs. Sadler has been picking on our Junior Hostesses ever since the Canteen opened. Of course, she's never gone this far . . ."

I stopped.

"*Most* of the captains will be angry. There'll be a few who will look uncomfortable, and shift nervously in their seats, and say, 'Well . . . er . . . Rabinowitz?' "

"Rabinowitz," Tom said, laughing, "is admittedly not a musical word. But when you come right down to it, neither is Higgins or Featherstonehaugh. Or Eisenhower."

"Mrs. Sadler is self-appointed. She can't be voted out of her position because she wasn't voted into it.

65

If we combined to send her a letter of protest, she'd tell the Governing Board we were all Communists and we'd be asked to resign. Some of the Board members might sympathize with us, but they're very sensitive to the fact that Mrs. Sadler could close the Canteen in half a day. She'd just have to take her money away. And her friends' money."

Tom laughed.

"You're so gullible, chum," he said ruefully. "Mrs. Sadler wouldn't close the Canteen if she had to take the affront direct in the Rose Bowl. She's got too big an emotional stake in it. She's known from here to Kansas as one of its founders, and she gets in the papers oftener than a promising shortstop."

He fumbled for a cigarette and lit it.

"The stars may lurch in their courses, but Mrs. Sadler won't close the Canteen until the war is over. Don't let her fool you."

I was silent, because I couldn't help seeing instantly that this was mathematically correct.

"Just the same," I said, after a moment, "that doesn't leave us any further forward. Suppose the captains wrote to her and asked for an apology on behalf of Mae. She wouldn't even bother to answer the letter, but she'd go around saying we were all Communists."

"Suppose she did?"

Tom shrugged.

"It wouldn't be true, would it, just because she said it?"

"No, of course not. But . . ."

Tom reached for a cushion and stuffed it behind his back.

"As long as I'm going to lecture you, I might as well be comfortable," he said. "The word 'Communist' is like the word 'bastard.' It started out as a specific label for a definite thing, but it's grown into a term of general abuse. If I get into a fight with a taxi driver and he calls me a bastard, he doesn't mean I'm illegitimate. He doesn't know whether I am or not. He just means he thoroughly disapproves of me. It's the same with Mrs. Sadler. If she says the Junior Hostess captains are Communists, she doesn't mean they belong to the Communist Party. She has no way of knowing whether they do or they don't. She just means she heartily disapproves of them. And Mrs. Sadler, like the taxi driver, hasn't got a very large vocabulary, so she has to get her epithets from the ready-to-wear department."

He shoved the cushion into a better position.

"What's in a name? If Mrs. Sadler had been a late Roman, she would have called you a bunch of Christians instead of a bunch of Communists."

"I can see what you mean," I said. " 'Sticks and stones may break my bones, but names will never hurt me.' Only names do hurt people. If we protest to Mrs. Sadler, we won't succeed in getting an apology for Mae. But we certainly will succeed in getting ourselves thoroughly labeled as agitators and trouble makers and Communists and what-all. A~ ¹

67

on, if we so much as sneeze in that Canteen, we'll be asked to resign."

"Suppose you are?" he said calmly. "The war effort is big enough so that you can find plenty of other things to do."

He must have sensed my dismay, because he went on.

"I know, Gretchen, I know. You've worked there a long time, and you love it, and you don't want to be asked to leave. But don't you understand that you'll never love it quite so much again, if you let this go by? It will be a place where things like this can happen and go unreproved. It won't be firm ground under your feet any more. It will be full of quicksands."

He got up and went over to the fireplace and kicked at one of the logs. Turning around, he said, "Mae Rabinowitz is an American citizen. American citizens have the right not to be singled out for insult on account of their religion. Mae didn't lose that right because Mrs. Sadler gave a lot of money to a canteen."

He stopped, and the room was entirely silent except for a little crackle from the fire.

"Fighting for democracy," Tom said gently, "isn't the exclusive privilege of tail-gunners."

I stood up.

"You win," I said, giving him a wobbly smile. "I'll do what I can."

I moved till I could see myself in the mirror over the mantel and took an absent-minded glance at my hair.

"But as a practical proposition," I continued, "it strikes me as being in the same class with going over Niagara Falls in a barrel. The only person who has any influence with Mrs. Sadler is Mr. Richards, and he's her spiritual twin. They work hand in glove on everything about the Canteen."

"Well, there you are! You get a committee of your Junior Hostess captains to go and see Mr. Richards. You flutter your eyelashes and your feather boas, or whatever it is women wear, and you ask wonderful, wonderful Mr. Richards to persuade Mrs. Sadler to write a note of apology to Mae."

"Little you wot," I answered sadly. "This Mr. Richards is a tough hombre. He's about as susceptible to charm as the Anopheles mosquito."

"However," I concluded, "I'll suggest it to the captains. I'll even ask if I can be put on the suicide squad."

"You won't be sorry," he said, and the way he looked at me made me feel very much pleased with myself. Not, of course, that it's a state of mind I put up any last-ditch resistance against falling into.

February 17th

Owing, brother dear, to the pressure of certain non-idealistic matters connected with the production of dinner, I wasn't able to finish my story yesterday. But I will now.

Everything has arranged itself with the speed and

69

dispatch which ensue when you inadvertently step down a laundry chute. First thing yesterday morning, Bonnie McKay called up. Bonnie is a trained nurse, about forty, small and wiry and brimming with so much practical, maternal energy that one suspects she was made by melting down two or three other women and distilling the residue. Unlike your ivory-tower sister, she loves a fight. Bonnie was thoroughly angry when she called, and I gave her just time enough to say she'd decided what we should do about Mrs. Sadler (put a propeller on her tail and launch her at a Jap transport), before I told her Tom's suggestion about the suicide squad. A lady getting a missing belt back from the cleaner couldn't have been more surprised and pleased, and she asked me why I had been keeping somebody like Tom under wraps—a query I allowed to go unanswered.

At Bonnie's suggestion, she and Lucy Carroll—who is head of all the Junior Hostesses and therefore Bonnie's and my boss—came over to our house in the afternoon. Lucy Carroll is a paradox. In most beautiful women you discover tiny flaws and blemishes as you get to know the ladies better, but in Lucy you keep discovering little perfections you hadn't noticed at first, the initial effect was so breath-taking. She's tall and dark, with grave eyes and skin so white and silken that it seems to operate without the intrusion of any tawdry elements like blood. Lucy is thirty, and it's quite evident that her looks are going to last until they start being impinged upon by daisies in a churchyard, but she isn't married and many a Junior Hostess with a face like a basket of mushrooms has more dates than she. I don't know whether it's because that self-effacing sex you belong to doesn't feel equal to carrying off the impression she makes, or whether it's that, outside of a portrait in oils, you never in your life saw such serene good manners and such matchlessly ladylike composure.

Lucy listened impassively while Bonnie and I told her—enlarging on several points in between—what Mrs. Sadler had said and what Tom had suggested.

"I think we'll do it this way," Lucy said. "I'll bring the matter up from the chair. Gretchen will tell what happened. Then Bonnie will get up and suggest . . ."— Lucy smiled faintly—"the suicide squad."

She picked up her tea cup so gracefully that I felt as if I were treating mine like a hand grenade.

"Then I'll suggest that the delegation be composed of you two, who were the witnesses, and myself, as head of the Junior Hostesses. Any more would be cumbersome."

"But what," Bonnie said, "about the captains who are going to say let's not do anything, it's apt to cause trouble, we mustn't get ourselves branded as agitators, and so on?"

"We'll let them talk themselves out," Lucy said comfortably. "There aren't enough of them to carry a vote."

So that's how it is, Jeff. For the sake of harmony— or a semblance thereof—in an organization we think does a lot of good, we've all submitted silently while Mrs. Sadler tried to mold the Junior Hostesses to her

71

arbitrary and unappetizing standard of American womanhood. But this time she went too far. I won't pretend I'm not scared. Lucy will stop at nothing to make the world safe for Junior Hostesses, and Bonnie is the sort of woman who thinks it's fun to take a whip and a chair and go into the cage with Westbrook Pegler. But I have to admit that I wouldn't have done anything about this if Tom Garrett hadn't cut off my retreat.

Bonnie says lightly, "What's the worst that can happen? Mr. Richards can say no." But she doesn't realize that we're about to touch off a reflex action. So far as the Canteen is concerned, Mrs. Sadler's money and her legendary meanness have enabled her to live in an egotist's dream world. When we go crashing into that dream with even the merest intimation that an apology is necessary, her reaction is going to be as unstudied and automatic as when you take a short stick and prod a skunk. However much you realize that the little creature can't help it, you still have to bury your clothes.

But I guess there's a silver lining, though to me it looks more like zinc. I guess I'm not going to have to worry for a while about letting life pass me by. I have an intuition that Mr. Richards and Mrs. Sadler are going to drop a good-sized section of it right into my lap. If you have any little old orisons you aren't using, Skipper, remember me in them.

Love,
Gretchen

72

Delightful Relative:

I was awakened in the middle of the night last night
by the noise of something falling. Reflecting on the
sound, I decided it hadn't been either Father or
the potpourri vases on the sideboard, and as those are
the only things for which I would get up out of a warm
bed, I went back to sleep. This morning I discovered
that some of the plaster had fallen from around the
leak in my bedroom ceiling. Ever since you went away
and bequeathed me the vain and thankless task, I've
been calling the real-estate company with pious regu-
larity about that leak. Sometimes they tell me it's all
my imagination and sometimes they say they will send
a man tomorrow. The last time they said they'd send
a man tomorrow, I said, "Don't bother about a man
tomorrow. Send me a little Dutch boy today, to put
his finger in it." The girl on the other end of the line
hung up.

I got the same girl when I called this morning.

"Oh, it's you," she said, in the tone of one who has
skipped the cold shower and the setting-up exercises.

I told her about the plaster falling, and pointed out
that one feature of a twelve-foot ceiling is that by the
time it hits you, it's really traveling. But the company
has apparently employed this maiden because of her
ability to ride the punches, and the prospect of my
tragic demise under several bushels of plaster left her
composure perfectly intact. She said she'd send a man
tomorrow.

Previous to going to bed cheek by jowl with the law of gravitation, I had had dinner at Janie's. Father had a meeting and couldn't go. He works so hard, Jeff, and I wish I could persuade him to take things a little more easily; but it would be like inducing a sledge hammer to loiter on the downward arc. Father is naturally intemperate, I guess, and all we can do is be thankful he's taken it out in work and reading. If he'd ever decided to go in for drink and allied self-indulgences, he certainly would have been a landmark in the history of excess.

But to turn to less worrisome things—you'll be glad to hear that Deborah has finally grown up to that big doll you somewhat prematurely gave her last year. Janie saves it for special occasions, and as soon as she opens the closet door, so that Deborah can see the box it came in, our niece goes into what I think is properly called a transport. She hugs herself, and wriggles like a sailor trying to get a nickel out of his front pants pocket. "Baby," she exclaims, "baby . . . ," and the accent is one of utter bliss. Infants, I note with envy, are receptive to enjoyment in a degree not attained by adults this side of the new Jerusalem.

Bill put Deborah and doll on the couch, and if you had seen her playing with it, my boy, you would have succumbed weakly to a batch of avuncular emotion. The doll's clothes are too complicated for Deborah to remove, but she claws off its bonnet and then puts it on again backward. "Baby" being all set for a little informal asphyxiation, Deborah strips off its shoes and

74

socks. (Through the whole process, she talks steadily, with the inflections and the intellectual content of a brook going over stones.) It takes her a minute or two to realize that she has about as much chance with the socks as she would with a Link trainer, but she can make the shoes stay on. It is apparently her idea that the success with the shoes is due entirely to the willing co-operation of the doll, so when she has gotten them on, she embraces it warmly around the head and rocks it back and forth, renewing the chant of, "Baby, baby . . ." This touching demonstration winds up with a long, wet kiss on the doll's cheek—a caress which would be more moving if it didn't remind Deborah that the doll's curls are, by her standards, edible, so that what started out as a sentimental gesture, ends up as a quick lunch.

Your present—I report wistfully—has been much more successful than something I gave her a few weeks ago. Passing through the Infant's Wear department at Altman's, I came across a pink bonnet lined, around the face, with tiny rosebuds. Don't try to wrap your rigid, masculine mind around this description, Jeff. Just take my word for it that nothing in the North Temperate Zone could have been better calculated to make Deborah look like a phantom of delight.

So, of course, I got it for her.

Last night I asked Janie if I could put it on her, to see what it looked like. Janie said doubtfully, "Well, she doesn't like hats much," but I, unskilled in the ways of tots, went and got it anyway. I hadn't even entered the room with it—Deborah couldn't have seen more than a flash of pink in the darkness of the hall—when she screwed up her eyes, opened her mouth till it would have caught the interest of a nesting swallow, and roared.

"*No* bonnet!" she screamed, and considerately sparing my intelligence any undue strain, she underlined the idea with a series of piercing shrieks.

I cringed against the doorway in the manner of one who has just been caught trampling on the American flag, and Deborah allowed her knees to buckle under her so that she arrived on the floor in a full crash dive.

"I guess she doesn't like it," I remarked nervously. Quick was the little maid's reply.

"NO bonnet!" she said, and placing her forehead firmly against the rug, she burst into a flood of tears.

I crept sheepishly away and restored my offensive gift to its shelf. When I came back, Bill was holding her, and her emotions had subsided to an occasional voluptuous sniff.

"Don't feel badly, Gretchen," Bill said. "It's just an idea she has. She'll get over it."

"Before people go around recklessly having children," I replied, "they ought first to see if they have any natural talent lined up in the way of aunts."

But really, Jeff, she's not a bit brattish or spoiled, in spite of the fact that she's an only child. After the bonnet had laid an egg, we played with her for a little while, and then, when she began to get overtired, Bill told her to come and sit down in her little chair, which was standing right next to his. She lowered her chin and looked up at him from under her considerable eyelashes with a glance which, I'm sorry to say, had more physical beauty than moral. There is no other word for it but calculating. Bill paid no attention and went right on talking. After a minute, when she had started moving craftily in the opposite direction, he interrupted himself just long enough to say, "Did you hear what Daddy said, Deborah?"

I thought Deborah was going to develop a split personality right in front of us, but in the end Filial Duty won, by the narrowest of margins, over Self-Expression. Deborah's gait could have been no more reluctant had her chair been modeled on the one at Sing Sing, but she finally got there. And once seated, she gave Bill a luminous stare, reached up to where his coat sleeve was lying on the arm of his own chair, and patted it magnanimously. Janie and I laughed out loud, and even Bill smiled, but he only ruffled her hair and went on talking.

Bill is as undemonstrative about Deborah as he is about Janie, and you know Bill—his idea of being wildly affectionate is to refrain from bending your fingernails back. But Deborah loves him to distraction, and whenever he's in the house, follows him around so closely that he has a perpetual appearance of being up to his knees in little girl. To Janie's attentions, when Bill is around, Deborah submits with nothing warmer than mere tolerance—a phenomenon which would break my heart, if I were her mother, but Janie accepts it with her usual benevolent aplomb.

The word "aplomb" brings me, by an inverse association, to the captains' meeting. Bonnie and Lucy and I launched our program as scheduled, and the first reaction was a group of sentiments about Mrs. Sadler which had obviously not been culled from Valentines.

The second reaction came from Trent Corwin. Trent has a beautiful, deep voice and the prim, meaningless good looks of a Dean of Women. She can show cards and spades to an International Harvester when it comes to efficiency, but competes with it on about equal terms so far as understanding human nature is concerned.

"Do you think it's wise," Trent asked melodiously, "for us to get ourselves known as agitators?"

At the word "agitator," the captains sat up alertly.

"*You* won't be known as an agitator," Bonnie answered. "Gretchen and Lucy and I are going to take the rap."

The captains relaxed, but some of them looked a little guilty.

Trent ignored Bonnie and continued smoothly, "I know we all regret this incident very much, but I think the main thing is not to have the Canteen split apart by factions."

Bonnie got to her feet.

"Trent says the main thing is not to stir up trouble in the Canteen. It seems to me the main thing is to

78

see that this sort of incident doesn't happen again."

That, Bro., was the beginning of the discussion. I'll spare you the formidable miscellany, and only say that, since I made the acquaintance of the Canteen, I have learned that the orators who told me democracy is glorious were holding something back. The democratic process, outside of oratory, consists of nothing more imposing than sitting way past lunchtime while a regrettably untaciturn female argues via her Cousin Elmer. It seems he went to Boston one time. He took the Fall River boat and got up early in the morning and caught a bus to Providence . . . The point, though, has nothing to do with when he was in Boston. The point is something vaguely epigrammatic he heard the following year in Schenectady. Oh, well. I suppose the treacherous beauty of Fascism is that, seen from a distance, it appears like a way of getting what you want without first having to convince a committeewoman that the experiences of her sister's best friend are inconclusive.

Anyway, the argument about the suicide squad went on longer than a costume novel.

At one point a little, thin, bedraggled person called Sally Owen jumped fervently to her feet. Sally makes us all feel ashamed because she probably works harder than anybody else in the Canteen, but she Loves Beauty and has an embarrassing habit of calling things "sheer poesy." (Once I asked Bonnie if Sally were married, and Bonnie said, "She's not exactly married, but she lives with a piece of old brocade.")

Sally exclaimed shrilly, "We can't do this. Mrs. Sadler is a *great* woman. She's one of the founders of the Canteen, and we can't hurt her feelings."

"Maybe not," I said, "but we can try."

The captains giggled.

Another captain restored us to sobriety by saying she agreed with Trent about not stirring up trouble in the Canteen because the Canteen was part of the war effort and our first job was to win the war—we could take care of the other things later.

A second lieutenant's wife took issue—a shabby, sweet-faced woman who leaves her two babies in a hollow tree when she comes down to work at the Canteen.

"Any woman with a family could tell you," she said, "that the things you're going to do later, never get done."

"I might paraphrase a little," she added. "If a thing is worth doing at all, it's worth doing now."

Some of the captains clapped, but Trent was not impressed. Trent isn't Jewish or Negro or Roman Catholic or shanty Irish or poor or married, and she quite honestly can't understand why the people who occupy these situations don't make a neater job of it. She came back to the point that we would be called troublemakers, and to my dismay, I saw that she was beginning to cut a swath with it. In vain Bonnie argued that from a George-the-Third's-eye view, General Washington was a troublemaker; and that the question was not whether you were a troublemaker, answer yes or no, but for whom and about what were you making trouble.

Trent was riding herd—there was no question about that—and for my part I was tired, utterly discouraged, and so hungry I could have eaten an old West Pointer.

"There's nothing I'd like better than to protest about this incident," Trent was saying in her bell-like tones. It was the fourth time she had said it, but a lot of the captains nodded and murmured approvingly.

"Oh, come off it, Trent!" said a brusque voice. "There are plenty of things you'd like better. Such as keeping your drag with Mrs. Sadler, for instance."

The interruption came from a dark, sallow girl I privately think of as God's Angry Woman. She's always on the side of the angels, but her manner is generally the manner of a blacksmith dealing with an anvil.

With the skill of long practice, Trent paid no attention to her.

"A lot of work has gone into this Canteen. We like to think it's done a great deal of good. It seems a shame to tear it apart with factionalism for the sake of one individual. Particularly . . ."

She stopped abruptly.

"Particularly one called Rabinowitz?" asked Lucy gently, coming into the discussion for the first time.

"Trent only likes people named Mary Queen of Scots," observed God's A. W. with malicious casualness.

The atmosphere was what might be imagined to prevail in the display room of the Hercules Powder Company.

"Trent doesn't know Mae personally," I interposed hastily. "Neither do most of you. Mae isn't anything special. She has a lovely smile, and a certain puppyish charm—she's popular with the servicemen—but she can be rather boring . . ."

"Your integrity does you credit, Gretchen."

Trent cut in suavely.

"But I'm older than you are . . ."—she paused to let this magnificent achievement sink in—"and I know that sometimes we have to compromise, however much we may want to cleave to the line."

She leaned forward and impaled me on her bright, sanitary glance.

"Do you really think it's worth it, Gretchen? To stir up dissension and quarrels and bad feeling, for a little girl you say yourself is boring?"

"Yes."

I knew that Trent was picking on me because she had me figured as the weakest link, and the only thing we had in common was that I had myself figured that way, too.

"Why?"

Everybody was looking at me, Jeff, and the Girl Scouts owe me a merit badge for the knots my stomach was tied in. I knew I was right, but when it came to putting it into words, I didn't know where to begin.

"Why?" Trent insisted.

From now on, Jeff, I don't want to hear any uncharitable remarks about the subconscious. Because an arm clothed in white samite popped up out of mine and it handed me Excalibur.

"Do you read the casualty lists in the *Times*, Trent?"

The captains turned as one woman and regarded her with interest. I thought everybody read them, but the heathen in his blindness could have seen that Trent doesn't and that she didn't want to say so. She cleared her throat—unmelodiously, I was happy to note—and I took pity on her and continued.

"The casualty lists are very thickly studded with names like Rabinowitz and Zablowski and Murphy and Vitello. They're not what some people call fine old American names. But they made fine old American soldiers and fine old American corpses."

"Oh, good! Good for you!" said the second lieutenant's wife, and her voice shook a little.

"We accepted their sacrifice, Trent," I said. "The wops and the sheenies and the harps, the Polacks and the Hunkies on the casualty lists. We didn't tell them not to go and fight, because we wouldn't protect their women from ungenerous persons while they were gone. They trusted us to take care of their people while they were away, even if it was forever . . ."

I heard a juicy little sound, and saw that Sally Owen was crying.

"Stupid of them, wasn't it? To think that we'd live up to our side of the bargain."

I knew I didn't have to go on, Jeff. I knew they were pawing the ground, waiting to give the suicide squad their collective blessing. But I suddenly got thoroughly angry with Trent for having cornered me and scared me so, and I thought that by golly, I'd rub salt in the wound.

"I'll tell you what we can do, Trent, if you don't want to stir up trouble. We can drop the whole thing about Mae Rabinowitz. We can just forget about it. But we can do something else instead that won't cause any dissension at all. We can have some little markers made for the graves of all the servicemen with the unfashionable religions and the jaw-breaking names. On the markers we can say, 'You should have stood in bed,' and we can sign it with the name of the Columbus Circle Canteen—that patriotic, morale-building organization which is uninhabitable for a good hostess because she's Jewish and her name is Rabinowitz."

In the stock phrase, Skipper, pandemonium broke loose. Not, I hasten to add, that pandemonium is any novelty at the captains' meetings. It has been known to ensue in a discussion over whether it is Tuesday or Wednesday. But this was a new high, even for Weaker Vessels in Congress assembled. Everybody talked at once, and Bonnie came over and kissed me. Several other people laid approving arms across my shoulders, and even Lucy, who can generally handle Chaos and Ancient Night with one tap of the gavel, had some trouble restoring quiet. The motion was made, seconded and passed that the suicide squad should go as a delegation representing all the captains, and even Trent voted for it.

Trent was pale and her hands were shaking. When

84

she voted for the motion, Bonnie said respectfully, "That's very graceful of you, Trent," and several people cheered faintly. But when I looked over at her, and saw her looking at me, I could tell from her eyes that she's never going to forgive me, and I promise you, Jeff, it give me a turn, it did. Trent is the reverse of a dope, and she carries a lot of weight around the Canteen. She can make things rather unpleasant for me, and as we go to press, she has not got any roses lined up to strew in my path. I keep telling myself that you can't make an omelet without breaking eggs, but so far as I know I've never had a real enemy before, and it's a thing I could easily do without.

But I didn't have any choice, did I? If people could never do anything except what is within the limits of Trent's sympathy and understanding, we'd have a nation solidly populated with well-groomed zombies. On second thought, thinly populated.

But I must bring this enormous letter to a close. I don't know why I go on at such length, except that—since you went away to take pleats in the enemies of the Republic—you've gotten more cozy and brotherly than you were the whole year before you left. In connection with brotherliness, however, I trust that in the future you will modify the lightness and flippancy of your attitude toward me. I trust that in the future you will take me more seriously. Because I'm the Pride of the Fifth Ward, Jeff, I'm the People's Choice.

Affectionately,

Gretchen

P.S. Don't mind me, I'm dragging my anchor.

85

P.P.S. Lucy and Bonnie and I had lunch together after the meeting, and telephoned Mr. Richards' office for an appointment. Mr. R. is a lawyer—member of a firm called Stanley, Pearce, Froman, Richards & Purdy. ("Take the ablative," I always want to add.) His secretary seemed somewhat surprised by our request, but said if it was about the Canteen, she was sure he'd see us. So we have an appointment, but not till the end of next week. I don't know what he's doing in the interim—probably playing squash rackets with a couple of hanging judges.

February 25th

Dear Jeff,

Up from the meadows, rich with corn, came the real-estate company's man-tomorrow, to look at my bedroom ceiling. Unfortunately, this artisan turned out to be a plasterer. He regarded me with envy and respect, as though wishing *he* had a collection of plaster that would come when you called it, but said we'd have to have a plumber to fix the leak first. I phoned the real-estate co., but made little progress against their conviction that I was splitting hairs. Plumbers are hard to get, they said aggrievedly, and suggested that if I were as true-blue as it said in my high school yearbook, I would have made do with the plasterer. I am patient with them, though. They may be causing me a little inconvenience right now, but I think before I am through, I can sell them Manhattan Island.

Your letter came this morning, darling, and I have been out carving it on beech trees that you are a sweet gent. I'm glad you think I'm blossoming out, and grateful (though not surprised) that you knew this was the precise, psychological moment for Brother Jeff to come through with a little reassurance. I have a deep-seated case of happiness that the captains are so solidly behind the suicide squad, but as our appointment with Mr. Richards draws nearer, I am increasingly aware that Mr. R. has very low ideals and does not handle well at thirty thousand feet.

Also, I wish I had arrived in this noble, if nerve-wracking, position by some handsomer method than propulsion from the rear by the man Garrett. The man Garrett is deplorably lacking in humility, Jeff. A gentleman who is not tall and who is one day going to be bald ought to manifest a decent degree of unease and insecurity about these shortcomings. But Tom Garrett is apparently under the impression that they are practically aphrodisiacs. It's annoying to be indebted—as I have to admit I *am* indebted—to someone who has all the quivering sensitivity of a Hubbard squash. When I was passing his room the other day, he called me in to give me a detective story he'd just finished. (He's the only human being I've ever known who reads as many detective stories as I do. Or as I did, before the war.) Gosh, remembering the way that room used to be in your day, I could have burst into tears. There were clothes on the floor; the lamp

87

shades were crooked; the ash trays looked like Mount Vesuvius after a busy day; and books and letters were lying around in the fascinating disarray produced by a wind tunnel.

"Well," I said, raising my eyebrows and looking pointedly around at the mess, "I see you're not bucking for corporal."

He laughed and stretched and yawned, after which he deliberately heaved three more books and a bathrobe onto the floor.

"That's the trouble with you Americans," he answered languidly. "You take too many baths."

A pox on him. He's gotten me into a bad mood. I'd forgive you for being skeptical, but I really did start this letter in a state of carbonated euphoria because you'd said such amiable things about Bonnie and Lucy and me. Unluckily, I haven't time to rewrite it, with more of an eye to Brightening The Corner Where I Am, because I have to go to the A. & P. for curds and whey. I have put next week's ration points in the sun on the living room window sill, but to date they haven't ripened up. I often laugh, these days, to think of the long talks you and Father used to have about my education. Of course, I know I rather spoiled things by marrying the Answer to a Distiller's Prayer instead of going to college, but you might at least have insisted on my taking an extension course in shoplifting. There seems to be no legal way we can get out of having oatmeal for dinner tonight.

Gee whizz, I *am* fretful, aren't I?

And this is not the way one is supposed to write to the boys in service, hein?

Forgive me. I'll add a few lines tomorrow, and I'll be so sunny and optimistic you'll have to analyze the fluff from my coat pockets to distinguish me from Pollyanna.

February 27th
Where-Neither-Moth-Nor-Rust-Doth-Corrupt-Department:

Do you know how badly I need a new hat, my son? How badly I need a new hat is that I'd accept a crown of thorns if it had a veil on it. This morning I got out a little number which must have looked awfully cute when I wore it to the Congress of Vienna, and took it down to my little woman to be cleaned and re-blocked. I stated firmly when I went in that I wasn't going to buy a new hat—I just wanted the old one fixed up—and the little woman swallowed this and licked the spoon. But just casually, by way of making small talk, she brought out a model which I would rescue from a burning house ahead of my opal ring.

It was a tricorne, and you might as well unglaze your eyes and simulate attention, because I intend to go through with this. A tricorne is a three-cornered hat, like the ones George Washington wore. The blue hat I bought for your wedding was a tricorne, and you went on saying it was mighty pretty for quite a while after I'd taken my four-inch heel off your instep.

89

Anyway, the one this morning was so dashing and bewitching . . . I can't tell you, except that if ever a piece of felt said airily, "Go jump in the lake!" this was it. The worst of it was that I have been secreting wampum in my dime bank with the idea of buying a War Bond, and I could have paid for the hat with that captivating staple known as hard cash. I didn't, though. "*No* bonnet," I said, even when the little woman followed me to the door with arguments which were sound, persuasive, and based on the theory that great oaks from little tricornes grow. I am now experiencing the elation attendant on the functioning of my better self, but every time I pass the hall mirror, on my way out of the house, I wince and think shudderingly that boy, I certainly am resistible!

The idea of being resistible brings me with a hop, skip and a jump to Mrs. Sadler and Mr. Richards, and your query as to how the Canteen happens not to discriminate against Negroes when those two are at the helm. I wasn't there when the place opened, and the no-discrimination policy was already organized and operating by the time I arrived, so all I had to do was step into it. But there is a group of people at the Canteen—quite a large group—which has no formal standing or title or recognized function. It just adheres. This group is called by Mrs. Sadler "the niggerlovers"; by Mr. Richards "the Reds and long-haired radicals"; and by itself the King's Own Subversives.

When the Canteen was being set up, it never occurred to Mrs. Sadler and Mr. Richards that anybody opening a structure for the armies of democracy would admit American citizens of color, whereas it never occurred to the King's Own that anybody wouldn't. The King's Own couldn't quite see themselves standing at the door and saying to a man in the armed forces, "Son, that uniform isn't good enough to get you in here." So Negro servicemen had been welcomed and Negro Junior and Senior Hostesses signed up, before Mr. Richards and Mrs. Sadler had finished obliging the photographers.

Once the Negroes were there, the Iron Twain didn't dare ask them to leave. It might have caused a jarring note here and there in the rapturous publicity the two of them were getting as suppliers of egg salad sandwiches to deserving heroes. They had no choice but to endure the situation with what grace they could muster, which was about enough to be comfortably accommodated on the head of a pin. Mrs. Sadler looks right through the Negroes and pretends they aren't there. Mr. Richards occasionally mutters that with all these blacks and whites around, there's going to be a raping some day. (A peculiar word for him to use, because his vocabulary is usually immaculately tailored.) There is a story that he said this once to a soldier, who drew back in surprise and exclaimed, "Why, you old goat!" The story is apocryphal, Mr. Richards being a lawyer of great renown, and too shrewd not to pick his spots better than that.

91

This is going to be a delightful evening, and I wish I could wrap up part of it and mail it to you. You'd like it. Father is at the Ration Board and Tom Garrett has gone out with a bunch of shy but virile-looking aviators who called me "Ma'am" and allowed as how this metropolis would no longer be virgo intacta by the time they got through with it. The air was warm and quiet today, as if it were getting into practice for spring, and I bought some daffodils which I have put on the lowboy in the Jensen bowl you gave me. Father will almost certainly knock them over, or at least spill some of the water, when he puts away his gloves. I am, however, going to leave them there just the same, on the principle that life is short, but art is long. (I leave you to imagine what a succès fou this explanation is going to have with Father.)

My blue bathrobe has just come back from the cleaner's, and I have my delicious, sensual, voluptuous rabbit's-fur slippers on. As soon as I've finished this letter, I'm going to lower myself solicitously to the sofa and spend the rest of the evening reading and not holding my stomach in. In connection with which: I've almost got my weight up to the requisite hundred and ten so that I can be a blood donor. I don't suppose it should be humiliating to be blackballed by the Red Cross, but it is. And in my case so needless, too, because it isn't as if I *used* that blood. It just stands around in pools. However, if they turn me down next time, I'm going to slash my wrists right in their front office.

Who do they think they're toying with, anyway?

I was passing the lab today and stopped in to say hello to Miss Ellsworth. Except that nobody ever gets away any more before seven in the evening, the lab is virtually unchanged. Roentzen is using your office, but has left it just as he found it, and the torch Miss Ellsworth carries for you is still burning with a hard, gemlike flame. Your white coats have been freshly laundered and are hanging in the locker against your return. Sometimes I think I ought to tell Miss Ellsworth that you aren't worthy of her selfless devotion, but I am always deterred by a mild suspicion that maybe you are. To Roentzen, the Misses Ellsworth, Stafford and Adelman refer with impatience bordering on contempt, but this is not entirely because he is so much less brilliant than you. It is also directly connected with his having four children and a mortgage in Montclair. That sort of goings-on makes a man's lady employees critical to the point of intolerance.

Those last four syllables remind me that I told Father at dinner tonight about Mrs. Sadler and Mae Rabinowitz and the suicide squad. I haven't mentioned it to him before because he's been too tired in the evening to listen, and I soon realized that it was very naïve (that's Bergdorf Goodman for stupid) of me to have mentioned it now. Father went to one of those grammar schools where they teach you that Americans are born tolerant the way some people are born with long eyelashes. You just emerge from the uterus in a geographical area labeled U.S.A., and there you are,

93

you're tolerant. Any evidence—that he can't escape by turning a page—to the effect that intolerant Americans exist, makes Father feel as awkward as if he'd gotten into the Ladies' Room instead of the Gents'.

He looked shocked when I repeated Mrs. Sadler's remark, but when I told him about going to see Mr. Richards, he said in a complaining voice, "I don't know, I don't know. With people like that, the best thing to do is stay away from them."

"That's what they're counting on," I replied cheerfully, and changed the subject. Father isn't getting any younger, and he's deserved better of life than to have me as the malaprop of his declining years.

Later on, though, I got to thinking how unspecific the word "tolerance" is. Except for suggesting vague inactivity, it doesn't really tell you much more about a person's character than the word "Mongolian." I've never dared describe myself as a liberal, for fear a voice from the gallery would say mockingly, "Who isn't?" but I would certainly have said that the mere fact of my being dismayed and horrified at Mrs. Sadler's remark proved that I was tolerant. Only, until Tom Garrett dug the spurs in, the person I was prepared to be tolerant of—i.e., inactive about—was Mrs. Sadler, not Mae.

Americans (I, I'm afraid, among them) go around carelessly assuming they're tolerant the way they go around carelessly saying, "You ought to be in pictures." But in the clinches, they turn out to be tolerant about as often as they turn out to be Clark Gable. Aunt Julie, for instance, can't even hear the phrase "religious tolerance" without acting as if somebody had just given her a corsage. She thinks she's got a corner on it, and she thinks it means maintaining a slumbrous lethargy while the Jews or the Roman Catholics or the Negroes build a church. Provided, of course, that they build it on the wrong side of the tracks. But if they propose to worship on the right side of the tracks, Aunt Julie springs into very unslumbrous action with the battle cry of "real-estate values."

One reason, Jeff, why I sometimes hope there will be a real, literal Day of Judgment is that my idea of Heaven consists of being in the audience when Aunt Julie explains "real-estate values" to God. I think she's figuring that He, having many mansions, will not prove to be unsympathetic; but the way I dream it, He's going to rub His hands together and say pleasantly, "Julie, old girl, if you'd changed the human values—which, since you were a human being, nobody was better fitted to do—the real-estate values would automatically have adjusted themselves."

Then He will turn to the nearest seraph and say, "Will you direct this lady to the wrong side of eternity? When it comes to keeping up the tone of the neighborhood, two can play at that game."

Oh, well, I don't own property, so it's no skin off my knees. What *is* skin off my knees is the Spartan implication of l'affaire Rabinowitz: That if you aren't willing to get into squabbles and take risks for what you believe, you might as well not waste any energy believing it. Either I'll have to admit that I don't really believe in anything except my own comfort, or I'll have to spend the rest of my life periodically incurring the bad will of people who have more force of character than I, like Trent Corwin and Mrs. Sadler. There may be graceful and eloquent ways of summing up this dilemma, but all I can say is, "Ugh!"

To conclude, however, on a pleasanter note: You will have noticed that I've taken your injunction not to count on the three-day pass so seriously that I haven't even mentioned it. As a matter of fact, I've already left it behind me and I'm speculating on whether they'll give you a furlough at the end of your basic. If you got a furlough, there's a spinster of this parish you could take some pictures of. Name of Deborah. In your absence, Bill and Janie had some done by a professional, but when Father saw them he turned to Bill and said politely, "What made you think of going to a taxidermist?" And that's really what they look like, compared to the ones you used to do.

You see what you are? Irreplaceable.

But I won't count on the pass, because from the way you describe your C.O., a soldier would get more of a break from a werewolf.

And that's the lot, boy.

Love,
Gretchen

Dear Kinsman,

You know what? This time last year I was importuning Providence to let something happen to me. Something a trifle more intoxicating to mind and spirit than discovering moths in our bathing suits. All I can say now is that if I'd known the dreadful efficacy of prayer, I would have kept my mouth shut.

I came home from the Canteen last night to find Father and Tom Garrett drinking beer and eating some cheese I had hidden away because I know the rapaciousness of my little brood and I wanted to use it today. That's one of the reasons I often wish there were some other opposite sex than yours. Why couldn't it be arranged? After all, when you think of what they do with fruit flies . . . I'd like somebody to breed a male, genus homo, who could go and fetch a 12″ x 8″ black suède purse lying in the middle of a white bedspread and not come back looking baffled and saying he couldn't find it. On the other hand, there should be omitted from the make-up of this sterling character those ductless glands which automatically guide him to the place of concealment of tomorrow's lunch.

Oh, well. That's the trouble with hitching your wagon to a star—nothing happens when you say, "Giddyap!"

Anyway, there was a driving rain last night, and after a brief struggle in the vicinity of my conscience about the gas and rubber shortage—additionally complicated by our family's legal tender shortage—I decided to take a taxi home from the Canteen. But when, defiantly self-indulgent, I got outside in the downpour, no taxis were vouchsafed. This should have pleased me, but failed to. I arrived home in a state which could have charmed nobody, with the possible exception of a merman, and Father looked at me and said stupidly, "Well, well, what have you been doing?"

"Ducking for apples," I answered waspishly, and went to change my clothes.

When I came back, I found Tom and Father on revoltingly good terms. Tom calls Father "sir," and listens to his time-worn anecdotes with respect and attention. Under the spell of our lodger's sycophantic appreciation, Father beams like a collie whose head is being scratched. To this, in itself, I would have no objection. But whenever *I* have any conversation with Brother Garrett, however gay and harmless it may be at the beginning, it always ends up with his telling me I'm refusing to face something or other. Since the things he says I refuse to face are always disagreeable in the extreme—such as that I'm too much attached to Father and I'm not making any emotional provision for my life after Father's gone—I think I show exceptional good sense in not taking them to my bosom. The bosom, after all, is a delicate and sensitive region, and comes up into blisters under mustard poultices and harsh, unseemly truths. It's difficult, though, to maintain this or any other position in the face of systematic taunts.

That, if I haven't gotten too far from the point, is why I do not look with the eye of love on Tom's and Father's entente cordiale.

Father told the one about the Congregational minister and the watermelon, and I made myself a highball. A little spiritus frumenti, I thought, might stimulate my feeling for the brotherhood of man. It did, too. Father said good night and went to bed, and I decided I would make an effort to be agreeable for the duration of my drink. I told Tom about having encountered Bonnie in the Canteen cloakroom—her knees buckling from an hour and a half of·hearing about the home life of a bassoon player.

"The reason Mr. William Saroyan is so fond of 'the little people,' " Bonnie remarked bitterly, "is that he's smart enough never to let them get a word in edgewise."

I also told Tom about the captains' meeting and our assignment to wait upon Mr. Richards and fill the wall up with our English dead. One thing I concede our lodger. He applauds with the same devastating wholeheartedness which informs his criticisms. Since anyone wishing to indicate that I have civic or other virtues can depend on unlimited co-operation from me, we had an interval of complete harmony. But it didn't last—an eventuality which may just possibly have been my fault. Praise from Sir Hubert or no, I was still annoyed at the way Tom defers to Father and reserves his bargain-basement psychiatry exclusively for me. Why, I asked him, didn't he spread both the deference and the psychiatry a little more evenly around the family?

"That would be silly," he said composedly. "Your father doesn't need any psychiatry, and you don't need any deference."

"It couldn't possibly be, could it, that you're afraid Father might give you your come-uppance?"

"Dear me," murmured Tom, "they told me the natives were friendly."

"If they did," I answered, "it was lousy reconnaissance," and turned on the radio. For once the news didn't adhere to its customary policy of always being ten minutes away. It came on almost at once. Tom listened, while I decided that nothing would allay my sense of defeat, depression and dissatisfaction except about four fingers of morphia. In the absence of this materia medica, there seemed no course but to call it quits and go to bed. But when the news was over, Tom, quite without preamble, asked pleasantly, "Gretchen, why haven't you got any beaux?"

You probably think, Skipper, that I drew myself up to my full height and said, "Aren't you being impudent?" Unfortunately, my full height doesn't impress anybody but gnomes. I have, nevertheless, drawn myself up to it in so many conversations with Tom Garrett that I'm beginning to have a permanent aspect of Queen Victoria Reviewing Her Troops. I have also suggested that Mr. Garrett is

(a) impudent
(b) intrusive
(c) vulgar
(d) coarse
(e) underbred

But nothing happens. He only looks pleased and interested, like somebody having his palm read.

Well, I haven't found his weak spot yet. But I warn you right now, Jeff, that when I do, my subsequent behavior is going to give the Marquess of Queensberry ulcers.

At any rate, when he asked me why I don't have any beaux, I only said, "Why don't you have any belles?"

"How do you know I haven't? I might be keeping them up my sleeve."

"I might be keeping some beaux up my sleeve."

"No," he said reflectively. "After all, I live here. I know."

I didn't answer. I was fingering my empty highball glass and wondering whether or not to have another drink.

"You're not repellent," Tom continued, "and your legs are semi-divine. In the nature of things, there ought to be a couple of young squirts around here with troth in their eye."

I decided against another drink. It makes me talk too much, and the way the conversation was shaping up, I could see that what I needed was not a drink, but a cleft palate.

"I see a lot of men at the Canteen."

"Ships that pass in the night. That's not what I have in mind."

"Is there a subject-changer in the house? I have a subject I want changed."

"I bet," Tom affirmed.

I resorted to stubborn silence, but so did my tête-à-tête, and after it had gone on long enough to put six children through college, I couldn't stand it any more and said, "Everybody's been drafted. There's no one around but you, and you're too . . ."

I didn't finish. Tom looked as if he were being entertained almost beyond his capacity to bear it.

"I'm too short," he said, grinning. "And my hyacinthine curls are not long for this world."

In spite of the fact that this was exactly what I had intended to say, I was so embarrassed I could feel my nerves curling like bacon over a hot fire.

"Of course," Tom went on, "*I* don't think I'm pretty, but that's what all my friends say."

I couldn't help laughing, and he asked hopefully, "Want to feel my muscle?"

"No," I said, with emphasis.

"I'm not tall enough for Mrs. Roosevelt, but she's bearing up under it very well. I'm tall enough for you, though, and you aren't bearing up under it at all."

"I mean to have six feet or nothing."

"Six feet is what you get when they bury you. You may have to wait till then."

I ignored this.

"Six feet or nothing. The best is none too good for our Gretchen."

"That's a schoolgirl's point of view. At twenty-six, you're a bit long in the tooth for that."

This endearing sentiment had an adverse effect upon my self-control, but I managed to reply with tolerable smoothness.

"I'll say that for Philip. He was pretty awful, but there were yards and yards of him."

"Oh, yes, Philip," Tom answered musingly. "The best was none too good for our Gretchen."

I remember Father's mentioning, Jeff, that apoplexy doesn't run in our family. Maybe it didn't, but it does now.

"You still haven't answered my question. How do you expect to get married again, if you never have any dates?"

"How do you know I want to marry again?" I said irritably.

Tom made a face.

"I suppose now you're going to tell me you've been too much hurt."

"Well, I have been," I said furiously, not soothed by the fact that this was precisely what I had been going to tell him. Only more subtly, of course.

"Philip drank, and all his friends drank, and perfectly dreadful things happened. He ran up bills that Father had to pay, and you just don't know, that's all!"

"Oh, I know, all right," he answered easily. "I've

been around a little. I've had almost as unsheltered a life as you have."

I wasn't giving him my full attention. I was determined not to cry, but the wayward protoplasm was getting out of hand.

"Everybody's been 'too much hurt' at one time or another. Only some people aren't such rotten bad sports that they won't pick themselves up and try again."

He chewed on the corner of his lip.

"You really worship the past."

With a judicial air, he added, "You're in love with that beastly little half-baked union you had. You don't want anything to take its place."

I don't know how to tell you the rest, Jeff.

I threw the empty glass at him. *I* did. Your sister Gretchen.

Every time I think I've touched bottom, and I can't possibly feel any more shame, new vistas of humiliation open up.

He dodged expertly, and the glass splintered against the bookcase back of the red chair.

"Right over the plate," he said admiringly. "You're well co-ordinated."

I thought I'd die, Jeffie. As a matter of fact, I even waited a split second for that beautiful event to materialize. But it didn't, and I gained—as they say in novels—my room. It was only when I heard the door closing behind me that I realized the glass was one of those lovely ones you and Ellen had. That tore it.

104

I cried. I cried until the front of my face was worn right down to the bone and my pillow was threatened with tadpoles. At one point, I heard my near-victim get his coat and go out. He never wears a hat. After a while, I went into the bathroom and took one of your sleeping pills. When I saw myself in the mirror— my hair was all out of curl and I looked like a stand-in for Medusa—I would have wept anew, except that my respiratory system had collapsed and wouldn't inflate any more.

But there was a small area of balm in Gilead. I remembered as I was getting undressed that Tom was scheduled to leave on a trip this afternoon, and I decided I would stay out of the house all morning until he was gone. I got into bed convinced that my former luxurious habit of going to sleep at night was destined to be nothing but a pleasant memory for the rest of my life, and the next thing I knew it was morning. It was not only morning, but I had slept through the alarm, the sleeping pill was apparently getting time and a half for overtime, and Father was dressed and asking for breakfast. When I went into the kitchen, I saw that the glass had been swept up and emptied into the wastebasket. As we sat down to eat, Father said, "What's the matter with you? Have you got the vapors?"

"I broke one of Jeff's good highball glasses," I answered, a reply which certainly gives me two legs on the trophy for World Champion of Misleading Understatement.

Since Father doesn't notice glassware, unless it has a hole in the bottom, he wasn't interested.

"Garrett's gone," he said.

I swallowed.

"I thought he wasn't going till this afternoon," Father said. "He's a pleasant young man. It's good for you to have somebody young around the house, now that Jeff isn't here."

"Peachy," I agreed.

The next time I count my blessings, I must remember to thank whatever gods there be that I'm not a cretin. When you consider what an obtuse family I come from, it certainly was a close shave.

Father left and I washed the dishes and started to make the beds. When I got to Tom's room, I found it in its usual state of advanced decomposition. There was a note propped up on the dresser. It said:

Uneasy does it. I'll be back.

Yrs.

T.

That was when I decided to let the beds go and write to you. I don't know what to think, Jeff. I feel as if I'll never be the same again, and I don't like it. I like it so little, in fact, that I would be on the verge of more tears, except that the man is coming with the laundry.

Love,

Gretchen

Jeffie, you fine broth of a boy—

Father has just departed, with a jaunty step and his hat tilted over one eye, to tell the envious gentry at the office that his first-born has been shooting for record and made Expert. Jeff, you couldn't have made him happier if you'd discovered radium. He tried to maintain a dignified composure, and when he handed the letter back to me across the breakfast table, he only said, "Tell The Deerslayer that's very fine." But when Bill telephoned a few minutes later, I realized that this is undoubtedly the finest vicarious experience Father has had in years. To my certain knowledge, he's never so much as hefted an M-1 in his life, but he talked to Bill as if he counted that day lost when he didn't let loose with a hundred rounds.

You would have been so much amused, Jeff.

And touched.

As for me, I'm staggered. Of course, I knew—from Ellen—that you used to cut quite a figure in those Broadway shooting galleries. But I always thought that was just one of the dubious rewards of eating carrots. I didn't know it was for real. Here I've been worrying about how poor Jeffie was going to get through the war, him so thin and refined and all, and you turn out to be one of the two most lethal guys in Company A.

Reason totters.

I wrote to you yesterday—didn't I, just!—so you wouldn't be getting this today except that I can't let the sun get over the yardarm without telling you how much your prowess has done for our chest expansion. Incidentally, I forgot to mention that I have sent you some candy. I certainly hope it proves satisfactory. I wouldn't like to have you draw a bead on me.

Respectfully submitted,

Gretchen

March 5th

Dear Bro.,

I've heard of soldiers who succumbed to erosion while trying to put through a phone call from Fort Bragg, so I really did appreciate your calling up. Still—pleased as I am that your recent triumph has inclined you to take a more gladsome view of things— I could nevertheless wish that you didn't find the Tom Garrett situation quite so comic. And if you've been thinking yourself for a long time that I was in a rut, why in Heaven's name didn't you say so? But of course, that's the way it is with families. No feeling for delicacy restrains them, when you forget to put salt in the potatoes, from comparing you unfavorably with Benedict Arnold; but if they think you're turning into a frustrated old maid before their very eyes, they're too high-toned and fastidious to say so.

Or didn't you know you were thinking it, until the Little Shepherd of Kingdom Come pointed it out?

If the poor man's Sigmund Freud is here when you get home, you'll scarcely be able to avoid meeting him and your curiosity will be amply satisfied. He did say, a while back, that if you got home while he was in town, he'd go and stay with some friends of his so that you could have your old room. Even I—not wholly an adherent of his—have to admit that this was thoughtful and considerate, and it would have been a bonanza for you. That sway-backed old couch in Father's room is getting to feel more and more like a saddle for a dinosaur, and Father's snoring grows to sound increasingly like a vacuum cleaner in heat. However, this handsome offer was made before my artless attempt to cut Mr. Garrett's face to ribbons, and he may not feel quite so generous towards our family now.

I guess I don't know which side your bread is buttered on.

Oh, dear, Skipper, I oughtn't to write you in this querulous vein. You have enough troubles, even assuming you get a degree of pleasure from having your chest stove in by the recoil from a Garand. The reason I'm querulous is that I'm so completely mixed up. That Tom put me on the right track about Mae Rabinowitz (of whom, more later), I concede gratefully. I'll even admit—with no more reluctance than I'd feel about being burned at the stake—that the Garrett entity was right in what he said on that memorable evening when I gave my arresting imitation of a discus thrower. (The intricate ethical question of whether I owe him an apology has caused me some concern. But let's not be too hard on me. He asked for it.) So anyway, I suppose I have to face the unappetizing reality, don't I? I suppose if I don't want to spend a lonely old age in a boarding house, I've got to arch my chest, give a hitch to my bustle, and start asking people slyly how they did on their Wassermanns. But I don't want to, Jeffie. I can't *tell* you how much I don't want to. I'm not Sweetheart of Sigma Chi material, and if I married Philip against grueling competition, it was only because I amused him and he was obsessed with being amused.

Sometimes I think I'd give anything to get back to my tranquil, pre-Garrett era, only I can't help remembering that I was disposed to be a little critical of that tranquillity when I had it. This leaves me with nothing to lean upon save the somewhat inoperable conclusion that although I don't know what I want, I certainly do want it.

But that's enough of that. What do I think I am, introspective?

I've launched the spring cleaning by dusting all the books in the living room and washing the shelves. In happier years, when Coline ministered to our library, I used to feel rather snobbish and complacent about having the living room lined with books. I thought it showed we weren't middle-class. Or, at least, not very. (I have affidavits to prove that it's a matter of complete indifference to the world at large what class we are, but I continue to worry about it just the same.) Right now, however, with every muscle aching and my bronchial tubes furred with dust, I'd be willing to compromise. Right now, I'd be willing to exchange the books for some less exacting symbol of elegance and distinction, like the Ark of the Covenant or a mink coat.

I seem to recall that I wrote you I was getting along splendidly without Coline, but the announcement may have been a little bit premature. There are, it turns out, a great many things Coline did that I didn't know how much time they took, syntax? I made up my mind to do the best I could and not worry, but whenever I sit down to read after dinner, I'm unhappily aware that the kitchen shelves need cleaning, the bureau drawers are in that state of studious disorder usually associated with scrambled eggs, and the bathroom curtains look as if some impulsive suicide had just used them to hang himself with. The trouble about not worrying, I discover, isn't the flesh being weak. The trouble is the nasty little spirit being willing.

I've been so unhandsomely self-absorbed recently that I forgot to tell you I had a letter from Coline last week. She's working in a factory in Bridgeport, and, like Sister Susie, sewing shirts for soldiers. She sends you her love, and wants you to know that if you are issued a garment of markedly superior workmanship, you are to understand it comes from her. She misses us, but she likes the factory work because she doesn't have to be on her sad, sad feet. I miss her, too—for herself, I mean, as well as in her professional capacity. I miss the heavy tread, and the high-pitched giggle, and I suppose never for the rest of my life will I know anyone who puts parentheses around indirect quotations.

Laundryman said (he can't find the towl)

now seems to me the natural way to write it. Her shrewd, irreverent comments about you and Father endeared her to me, too. I often used to think that if you two gentlemen had had any idea of what farcical characters you seemed to Coline, you would have paid her off instantly and hired Cotton Mather instead. I find that I even miss the long struggle, none the less intense for being wordless, over whether the furniture was going to go where I wanted it or where Coline wanted it. I still think that, given time and perhaps the barest soupçon of assistance from the Marines, I could have won that fight.

There have been two developments in the Mae Rabinowitz business. Development No. 1 was that last week Trent Corwin resigned from the Canteen. We were all startled, and I personally felt the way you do when you go to lift something you think is heavy and it turns out to weigh nothing at all. Trent's official reason for resigning was that she has so many other kinds of war work, her health won't permit her to continue at the Canteen. She confided privately to a few indiscreet friends, however, that the organization is dominated by a group of people—some of the Junior Hostess captains in particular and the King's Own Subversives in general—who are disreputable, ill-educated, undiscriminating, and generally ignorant of the basic canons of good taste.

("Who, me?" Bonnie said.)

Trent allowed as how she had never been able to set foot in the Canteen without feeling J. Stalin's hot breath on her neck. For my part, Trent Corwin's neck is the last place in the world I'd look for impassioned exhalations, even from persons less notoriously composed than Comrade Stalin, but I suppose if a lady says the Communist Party has been eyeing her lustfully, it isn't polite to express any doubt. I suppose one can only say, "Well, well, opposites attract," and hope it doesn't sound too hollow to get by on.

In all justice, though, we'll miss Trent. She had a genius for systematizing things, and the Canteen is full of devices and routines—sensible to the point of being inspired—that Trent thought up and put into operation. As long as the place is open, people will be saved a lot of time and trouble because she was there. But it's the sort of thing that seems to happen frequently to people who are brilliant at handling inanimate objects, like nuts and bolts and balance sheets. "Now we'll just take and apply this to human beings," they say—eyes sparkling ambitiously—and they never get over a sense of outrage that they got their arms laid bare to the bone.

Development No. 2 was that the suicide squad went to see Mr. Richards. After we reached the premises occupied by his firm, we had a long wait before we were shown into his office. Mr. Richards' office is a big room with a cold north light to match Mr. Richards' cold north face. There are very small etchings in very big mats hung at sparse intervals around the walls, and the whole setup makes you want to rush right out and do something jolly, like compounding a felony.

Lucy did the talking. Mr. Richards would probably fall on his sword if he suspected himself of a thing so weak and degrading as a partiality for anybody, but whenever Lucy is around, he goes out of his way to talk to her.

Lucy explained our errand with such dignity and eloquence that Bonnie and I began to glow with optimism, even though Mr. Richards was leaning back in his chair and indulging in his customary pursuit of looking curdled. But when Lucy had finished, Mr. R. pushed out his lower lip thoughtfully and remarked, "Don't believe she said it."

Lucy caught her breath and I sat up, bristling, but Bonnie only laughed.

"You cannot always sometimes tell,
    Perhaps little pussy *fell* into the well,"
she said.

"That finishes it," I thought despairingly, for Mr. Richards is a mammal who seems more likely to be hardened than softened by light quips. To my surprise, however, he glinted appreciatively at Bonnie from under his eyebrows, of which he has thousands.

"Mrs. Sadler's private opinions are her own."
The inflection was unmistakably mocking.

"Oh, of course," agreed Lucy. "Only this one wasn't very private, was it?"

Mr. Richards sat up in his chair and rested both hands on the edge of his desk in a gesture of dismissal.

"I'm very sorry, young ladies, but I'm afraid I can't help you. The whole thing is a tempest in a teapot. Mrs. Sadler has been generous to the Canteen—extremely generous—and I don't want to trouble her with any such trivial business as this."

He started to reach toward a row of buttons on the side of his desk—presumably to summon whatever dignitary he employs when he wants people taken home on their shields—but Lucy interrupted.

"You say it's a trivial business, but could you tell us just one thing? Why is it trivial?"

I think, Jeff, he was on the verge of replying, "Because I say so," but he checked himself. He didn't exactly grow paternal, because it's impossible to imagine him fathering anything that isn't in escrow, but he got a little more expansive.

"It's trivial because of the relative positions of the people involved. If it weren't for Mrs. Sadler's liberality, there wouldn't be any Canteen. Most people would agree with me that she deserves every consideration."

If Mrs. Sadler deserves every consideration, then perhaps we've all been too hard on Jack the Ripper, but Bonnie and Lucy and I didn't say anything.

"On the other hand," Mr. Richards continued, "what has this little Mae What's-her-name ever done for the Canteen? Gone there and had a fine time with a lot of clean-cut young American boys she'd never have had a chance to meet if it hadn't been for Mrs. Sadler."

Bonnie wrinkled her nose.

"I'm afraid you'll have to do better than that."

Mr. Richards regarded her impassively.

"I beg your pardon?"

"You're not clean-cut, Mr. Richards," Bonnie said. "And I'm not, and Gretchen isn't. The only person in this room who's clean-cut is Lucy, and she's one in a thousand."

Mr. Richards surveyed Lucy lingeringly. A faint pink came up into Lucy's cheeks, and she bit her lower lip, which is a ripe construction and one that practically anybody would be glad to sink a tooth into.

"One in two thousand," said Mr. R., with the wary little snarl he uses to signify good nature.

"Remember you said that," Bonnie answered. "I'll hold you to it."

Mr. Richards' smile faded abruptly.

"Clean-cut-ness," Bonnie said, "is such a rarity in this country that Powers and Conover models get paid five and ten and fifteen dollars an hour, just for being that way. Not for singing or dancing or acting, but only for holding still and being clean-cut."

She picked up her gloves, smoothed them out, and laid them down again.

"Shall we not waste any time on how Mrs. Sadler

116

procured . . ."—she dwelt on the word—"clean-cut young men for Mae Rabinowitz?"

Mr. Richards was not at all discomposed.

"You're very clever young ladies. I'll even go so far as to say you're entertaining. But the fact remains that you can't do anything about this fancied slight, and you'd better just drop it."

When people are engaged in being well-intentioned, Kinsman, I always think it's very rich and beautiful if they can also be intelligent; but on the score of intelligence, the suicide squad certainly gets the Navy "L" for lousy. We should have seen right away that it was hopeless, and left. Instead, we stayed for almost an hour and accomplished nothing—except to provide a cynical, loveless and unimaginative old man with more gentle relaxation than he's had since he gave up pulling the wings off flies.

Mr. Richards loved it. He was particularly amused by our pretentious innocence in thinking we knew anything about the practical implications of democracy. Mr. Richards' forebears, he divulged, barked their shins on Plymouth Rock—a misadventure which, though it may have annoyed them at the time, had the benevolent result of making Mr. Richards an hereditary expert on democracy.

Only once, in all that weary enterprise, did we manage to get under his skin. Mr. Richards, in sportive mood, was assuring Lucy that he was grieved and surprised to find that she had let herself be taken in by the Reds and long-haired radicals at the Canteen.

(The taking-in of Bonnie and me, I am sorry to report, didn't seem to strike the ancestral democrat as much of a loss.)

With sardonic melancholy, Mr. Richards wanted to know how Lucy could lend the prestige of her very superior person "to a bunch of crackpots who spend their time kowtowing to the riffraff."

Lucy objected mildly.

"I don't know what you mean by 'riffraff.' "

For a moment, I was surprised. Lucy knows perfectly well what Mr. Richards means by "riffraff." He means Negroes, Jews, the foreign-born unto the third generation, poor whites, Roman Catholics, enlisted men and Mrs. Roosevelt.

Then I couldn't help smiling. Mr. Richards didn't seem to be troubled by any headlong impulse to say what he meant by "riffraff."

A small pause developed.

Bonnie ended it by turning to me, laying her hand on my arm, and asking solemnly, "Gretchen, what is 'riffraff'?"

I could see that she was faintly hysterical. So was I. Lost causes, apparently, have a deleterious effect upon the nervous system.

" 'Riffraff,' Mrs. Bones, is people without any background."

Bonnie widened her eyes.

"You mean, like Abraham Lincoln and Babe Ruth?"

"Yes, dear."

I turned to Mr. Richards.

118

"It's a syllogism," I explained helpfully. " 'Riffraff' is people without any background. Abraham Lincoln and Babe Ruth hadn't any background. Therefore Abraham Lincoln and Babe Ruth are 'riffraff.' "

"The people you mention," snapped Mr. Richards, "happen to have records of distinguished achievement."

It was the first time, Bro., that we'd made a dent in his amused condescension, and it was sweeter than the honey, *to* the honey bee . . .

I turned back to Bonnie.

"Revised definition, Mrs. Bones. 'Riffraff' is people without any background and no record of distinguished achievement."

Bonnie shook her head.

"A hundred and thirty million Americans," she said, in a mournful cadence, "and almost all of them 'riffraff'!"

Lucy shot her a look surpassingly demure.

"And what," Lucy asked, "is background?"

Bonnie took a deep breath.

"Background . . . ," she began, but Mr. Richards interrupted her.

"Let's get down to earth," he said dryly. "This sister act is not without charm . . ."

He made us a satirical little bow.

"But your martyred heroine could perfectly well go back to the Canteen."

I saw with dismay that if there had been, for a moment, a chink in Mr. Richards' armor, it was already neatly sealed over with New-Skin.

"Those people," he stated pleasantly, "aren't as sensitive as you think."

"There's no way of telling how sensitive people are." Lucy spoke with some heat.

"For all we know," Bonnie said, "even *you* might be sensitive."

"Though," she concluded, "it's certainly the least promising theory I ever heard of."

Mr. Richards looked pleased.

"I don't wear my heart on my sleeve, for daws to peck at."

"You could," I said. "The birds wouldn't touch it."

Mr. Richards looked even more pleased.

"You're too kind. But to get back to your martyred friend. You'd better just drop it. There's nothing you can do."

Shortly after that, we left, filing awkwardly out while Mr. Richards looked after us with a cramped but triumphant smile and murmured that if we had given our Jewish friend an exaggerated sense of her own importance, surely it wasn't his responsibility?

The suicide squad made a silent trip back to our house, furnished itself with Coca-Cola, and brooded gloomily over the unblushful Hippocrene. But in a little while our bulldog tenacity began to reassert itself, and we wrote a letter to Mrs. Sadler for the captains to sign. It was a voluptuously tactful production. We began by recalling the incident without mentioning specifically what she had said. We only remarked that, "unfortunately, it hadn't made a uniformly felicitous impression." We dwelt on how tired everybody was from war work and enlarged lyrically on how super-fatigued Mrs. Sadler must be from her unremitting endeavors. We really laid it on thick, Jeff. Nobody was ever coaxed into the nuptial couch with a more ornate tenderness than we expended on deflowering Mrs. Sadler's virgin self-esteem.

Our resurgence of hope and energy didn't blind us to the fact that the Scourge of Columbus Circle was most probably not going to reply to the captains' flower-decked communication; so we decided that we'd give her a week, and then we'd take the same letter and get it signed by all the Junior Hostesses—or as many, at least, as we could persuade of the rightness of our cause. Lucy said she would call a Junior Hostess meeting for the 14th. (It is the custom to have periodic meetings of all the Junior Hostesses—to remind them not to chew gum, listen to military secrets, or drop paper towels down the toilets, and to suggest, as delicately as may be, that they wear undergarments which restrain but do not provoke. Uplift brassières and tight sweaters disturb both the Senior Hostesses and the boys in service, though not quite in the same way.)

Then we called Mae Rabinowitz and told her to let us know if, by some miracle, she heard from Mrs. Sadler. Bonnie did the telephoning. As she listened to Mae, she began to look self-conscious. Putting her hand over the mouthpiece, she said apologetically to Lucy and me, "The child approves of us."

A moment later she said, "Oh, it's nothing. I

121

mean, it's something, but it isn't as much as that."

After another brief pause, she laughed.

"Never could stand a Sadler in all my bo'n days," she drawled. "Hit makes my blood bile to look at a Sadler."

Then she said good-by.

And I will, too, since this letter is already so long that I fear it will seriously discommode the Pony Express. Take care of yourself, dearest coz.

Affectionately,
G.

Dear Jeff,

I always read your letters attentively, but seldom have I perused anything with such loving care as I did your description of the lieutenant. If he is as handsome and as sweet as you say he is, my reaction can be summed up in the terse phrase, "Poppa, buy me one of those."

The King's Own Subversives divide Southerners into two classes—the silent South and the screaming South. In the silent South they include all the Southerners, like the charming loot, who are beginning to realize that two world wars for democracy in the space of thirty years have made the South's traditional attitude toward the Negro distinctly old hat. Since the silent South learned this attitude thoroughly, when it was wriggling little babies, its position—as you noticed in the lieutenant—is painfully productive of unease.

The screaming South, in this lexicon, is the one that gets its speeches on white supremacy reported in the New York papers, to the somewhat stupefied amazement of the subscribers.

You say, Jeffie, that it's all very well for me to be so irritatingly rational about the South, but I've never been there and seen it. Well, of course, I see only the export product, but they do not think of themselves as any the less Southerners because they are up here. Neither, I may add, do I. It isn't that I'm an apologist for the screaming South. (Not with *my* scar tissue!) I think the screaming South misstates its case, which is not so much that Negroes are an inferior race, as that *somebody* has got to be inferior and the Negroes are the handiest. If every single Negro were spirited out of the South tonight, by sundown tomorrow the screaming South would have made "inferiors" out of the telephone poles. Some day when you want to give yourself the horrors, Bro., try to imagine the South if all the Negroes suddenly packed up and left. The ensuing spectacle would suggest millions of dope addicts suddenly cut off from their drug.

But one point must be conceded to even the least pride-inducing elements in the South. When they say that if we Northerners are such a bunch of smartypants, why don't *we* do something about the American Negro, they've got us dead to rights. There's one thing a lot of us at the Canteen have learned, Jeff, and not in ten easy lessons, either: It's just a waste of time to preach racial equality to Southerners, because it doesn't mean the same thing to them that it does to us. To Southerners, racial equality means—not that the Negro would have his rightful, legal share in the life of this country—but that white Southerners would have to change places with the Negro. In the mind's eye of a Southerner, racial equality is racial, all right, but it certainly isn't equality. Consequently, the more you tell them that they must accept Negroes as equals, the more they dig their heels in and reply, "Says who?" You would, too, if you were seeing the same specters they are.

I come back to what you must, by this time, regard as my King Charles's Head: That the idea of equality—for everybody, including white Southerners—will have to filter into the South gradually, over a long period of time, and it will have to filter in from other parts of the country which are not themselves lazy and timid and prone to easy self-congratulation.

As far as your discussion with the lieutenant is concerned, I should (up to a point) have sided with him instead of you—and only partially because he is described as rangy, beautiful and drawling. I believe him when he says that the Negroes on his father's farm are the happiest people he's ever seen. A primitive, irresponsible life must have a lot to recommend it—as you would know, my son, if you had to polish all the candlesticks in our not sufficiently lowly cot, or else watch them turn black because there's no time to polish them. The fatal flaw in the lieutenant's father's arrangements is not, it seems to me, that his farm hands lead a primitive life. Explorers at the North Pole lead a primitive life, too; but they chose it. The lieutenant's father's employees had it imposed on them from the outside, and they are not encouraged—shall we say?—to escape from it. That's why the "Northern agitators" can stir them up with the flick of a finger, and make them, as it is generally phrased, act like damn fools.

Suppose by a miracle some other part of the country could be transformed overnight into a place of complete equality for Negroes. The lieutenant's father's farm hands would stream up to it in a body, and in a week or two, most of them would stream right back. But after that, the "Northern agitators" wouldn't be able to stir them up, because their way of living would have become the result of their own personal experience and their own personal choice. I rather suspect, from having seen Southern Negroes at the Canteen, that the white man's civilization is nothing to fool around with until you've learned how; and I think there must be a great many Negroes who don't realize the price we pay for our advantages in nervousness, insomnia and unremitting strain. I imagine it will take several hundred years for all the Negroes in the United States to be geared into the white man's society. Maybe some of them never will be. But their not being geared in will have to be their own decision, not anybody else's.

In the meantime, there's no pathway into the predominant civilization of this country—not really *into* it, only here and there to the edges—for even the brainy and ambitious Negro who is prepared to take the bitter with the sweet. And in the meantime, too, as long as we put off making a beginning of the gearing-in process—because of the initial effort involved— we keep feeling guilty and afraid. I can tell you this, Skipper. The only way not to worry about the race problem is to be doing something about it yourself. When you are, natural human vanity makes you feel that now the thing is in good hands.

Anyway—in despite of you, Jeffie dear—I string along with the lieutenant about the happiness of his father's farm hands and also about the unflagging kindness practiced toward Negroes by the best type of Southerner. I don't question, as you do, the existence or the quality of the kindness; but I think the mention of it is anti-climactic. It's rather like hearing a man boast that he can do one push-up. Because when you've got people as helplessly lashed to the mast as the Southerners have got the Negroes, you'd have to be extremely brutal and degenerate not to be kind to them.

Your letter gave me, as they so often do, a great twinge of desolation that we have to write all these things out, instead of being able to talk about them. If you were here, the lieutenant would have engaged us until so late that Father would have come bumbling out, during one of his wakeful spells, to enjoin us against ruining our respective healths by never going to bed. (Some day I'm actually going to go to bed when Father thinks I ought to, and let him see for himself that eight hours of sleep makes me droop like a plant with cutworm.) An odd thing is, Jeff, that the part of the lieutenant's discourse by which you were rather awed is the part with which I am not impressed at all—i.e., the South's much-touted bitterness about the War Between The States.

Don't furrow your pretty brow about it, feller. The Southerners of our generation didn't live through the Civil War. Neither did their fathers and mothers. Neither, except possibly as infants, did their grandfathers and grandmothers. That so-called bitterness has no immediate meaning to them. It's a completely artificial feeling with which some Southerners like to reinfect themselves, from generation to generation.

Since they—or some of them, anyway—elect to behave in that fashion, there's no way anybody can stop them; but we can at least refuse to be exploited by a pseudo-emotion that is utterly unconnected with any direct experience. The "bitterness" of the South, Jeffie, is purposely implanted—in children who would not otherwise have had it—to screen the fact that Poppa and Momma have not themselves done a hand's turn about the South's prevailing ill health, stretches of poor soil, and other local headaches. The young Southerners who are "bitter" could get over it in nothing flat, if they wanted to. That they don't want to indicates a human and understandable—but certainly not very romantic—desire to postpone the painful job of self-improvement.

But I'm speaking with a degree of asperity, and it isn't necessary. Because I can wait. I can bide my time as well as the next one. When the five thousandth Southerner—I'm only in the forty-five hundreds now— tells me that his sainted mother reached the age of eighty before she knew damyankee wasn't one word, I'm going to abandon my customary moderation of speech.

"Not really!" I'm going to say. "Provincial old bitch, wasn't she?"

By the simplest of modulations, this leads me to the fact that Aunt Julie was here for dinner last night. It seems to me that there is nothing in all human experience more surprising than the people you find yourself related to. By blood, to cap the climax. I don't mind Aunt Julie's having all that money. I don't mind her having babied cousin G. so much that the Army took one look at him and turned away with a polite vomiting motion. But when she wormed her way into our family, that was going too far.

Dinner started unobtrusively enough, with Aunt J. telling me for the millionth time that I ought to wear brown, because I have brown eyes, and with my replying for the millionth time that there is no use accentuating my already unfortunate resemblance to Jenny Wren. After that came the delicate job of trying to keep her off the subject of the President. Father did everything but stand on his hands, and I fluttered along in front of her, feigning a broken wing, but it was of no avail. She began discussing—if that is the word—the Chief Executive, and the Progenitor and I were flattened like reeds in a storm. There isn't any way you can argue with her, because the real reason she hates the President is that she suspects he gets more fun out of life than she does. Though he can't have had to strain a ligament to do that.

Over the dishes, she sobered off and we were serenely domestic. To do Aunt Julie justice, she is much nicer about helping with the dishes than another relative of mine, who shall be nameless. *She* doesn't hide behind the garment bags in the hall closet, and only emerge— all dewily surprised—when the broken meats are completely disposed of. If you want it straight from the shoulder, old boy, it's the way you say, "Oh! Why didn't you call me?" that has me showing the whites of my eyes.

When we got to the pots and pans, I started to put Dutch Cleanser into the skillet. In great alarm, Aunt Julie begged me to cease and desist. It is her theory that if you leave the grease in peace, it makes things taste better.

"That's the way it goes," I said. "First you send your children to progressive schools, and the next thing you know, you aren't scouring the frying pan."

Father, who must have been listening from the living room, said, "Hah!" but Aunt Julie only remarked, in honest bewilderment, that cousin G. had only been to a very few progressive schools and she never liked them.

When the dishes were done, Aunt Julie tuned up her

lyre and started in on the New Deal. Father undisguisedly read the paper, and I speculated on why Aunt J. should have such a maniacal sense of personal involvement about something in which her actual involvement was well within the limits of human endurance. I finally decided that it's a case of misplaced emotion. Aunt Julie thinks the New Deal clipped her wings, whereas in reality she clipped her own wings, years before Roosevelt was ever heard of, by being quick to criticize, harsh in her judgments, and so rapaciously timid she wouldn't let cousin G. walk around the block alone. But the New Deal suggests wing-clipping, and it gives Aunt Julie a wonderful chance to think that her unfulfilling life and her disappointing son are somebody else's fault, and not her own.

It's high noon, Sugarplum, and if I don't get something to eat within the next thirty seconds, I won't answer for the consequences.

Adios,
G.

March 15th

Dear Jeff,

Spring is giving us the old one-two. It's been the kind of day which makes a lady want to put vine leaves in her hair and be off over the hills in quest of something more or less in the Gary Cooper line. Responsibilities of a domestic nature interfered with

130

this delightful project, but I did my shopping with my coat recklessly flung open to the silky air and bought pussy willows for the living room. When I got home from the stores, I found that my spring clothes (if such a skimpy, spindling aggregation deserves the plural) were just pushing their little heads through the warm brown earth, so I tried them on. It was nice to see myself in something different, though anybody who wants the services of a hard-working, conscientious opium smuggler can have mine—in return for my not having to wear that navy blue coat another season. But I shouldn't complain. Not when I think of all the people who are modeling battle dress.

The soft air and the rising sap, though they have somewhat demoralized me, have had no such debilitating effect on the old man. I was delayed at a Canteen meeting this afternoon, and Popsy got home before I did, to an empty house and no sign of dinner.

"What was the matter?" he said, when I finally appeared. "I thought you'd outgrown me."

Aside from springtime, the only pretty ringtime, things are going on about as usual. The leak in my bedroom ceiling hasn't been fixed yet, but this morning an individual called on me and announced reluctantly that he was the plumber.

"Goodness me!" I exclaimed. "I thought you were extinct, like the buffalo."

He gave me a startled glance and seemed about to retreat, but I pulled him in and exhibited my cancerous ceiling. He was in mufti, without his overalls or tools, and had only come on a scouting trip; but I was so glad to see him I had to exercise considerable restraint not to ask for a lock of his hair.

He eyed the ceiling in silence for a while, and then went upstairs and accused the tenants overhead of steadfastly letting their bathtub overflow—a charge which they did not cuddle up to. Coming back down, he said he would have to have the superintendent's tall stepladder, to make a close inspection. Unluckily, the basement was locked and the super nowhere to be found. That is to say, he was probably to be found on Third Avenue, helping Connolly's & Donnolly's Bar & Grill to keep body and soul together. But the plumber seemed less a devotee of the primrose path than an admirer of the Methodist Board of Temperance and Morals, so I didn't suggest that he combine business with pleasure and go after the super.

He said he would come back at nine o'clock tomorrow morning, when the super is sure to be here because that's when he collects the garbage (except on the days when he decides to give us a touch of the whip and just leave it there). Previous experience with the real-estate company's hirelings makes me a little pessimistic about the plumber's keeping the tryst, but at least it's a step in the right direction.

Apropos of the right direction—yesterday we had the meeting of all the Junior Hostesses, to get them to sign the letter to Mrs. Sadler. There was a brief captains' meeting first, before the girls started coming in, and I could see right away that if Mrs. Sadler had been smart, she would have sent some sort of reply to the captains' letter, however negative. There seems to be something about having his communications ignored that gets a human being thoroughly sore, and even the captains who had been lukewarm in the beginning were now pulling on the traces.

We had about three hundred Junior Hostesses at the meeting, which is only half the total number, but it's all we ever get. There are many ways in which the Canteen reminds one of a democracy in microcosm, and one of them is that a lot of the citizens think E Pluribus Unum is Latin for "Let George Do It." The opening formalities having been dispensed with, Lucy asked me to describe the Rabinowitz affair so far. When I reported Mrs. Sadler's remark, the Junior Hostesses stirred and murmured, but when I concluded by saying the captains would like all of them to sign the same letter, they looked at me with surprise and distaste. I could see that they would have found me much more engaging if I'd asked them whether their scalps could pass the fingernail test.

Lucy followed me immediately with a little speech she had prepared beforehand. It was a handsome talk—well organized and economical—but I had a feeling the audience was sliding out from under it. Lucy made too many stately threats about what would happen if prejudice were allowed to go unchecked, and the hostesses were not in the mood for warnings, however succinctly phrased. I began to get increasingly uneasy. There would, of course, be a handful of the girls who would sign the letter instantly, but a handful wouldn't do us any good. We needed the whole works.

Lucy had just reached her peroration when a chair scraped on the floor and a girl's voice exclaimed shrilly, "I won't sign the letter. I think it's all a bunch of nonsense and I think Mrs. Sadler was right."

There was a conglomerate squeak as all the girls in front of the speaker slued around on their undertaker's chairs to see what she looked like. She was tall and painfully thin, with a Hapsburg cast of countenance, and nothing about her suggested the ripe pomegranate.

"I wish somebody *would* clean the Jews out of this place," she said, her voice climbing. "And I don't care if there are Jews here right now. I don't like them and I don't care who knows it."

Three hundred people making no noise, Jeff, is a very peculiar sound.

The silence was broken by a good-natured laugh. It was Bonnie. All the girls who had been craned backward snapped around to the front again.

Bonnie crossed her legs casually and said to the Hapsburg girl, "That's too easy. It's what they call a mug's game."

The Hapsburg girl was dressed with some pretensions to elegance—she had a full-length silver fox coat that had certainly not been kicking around since before Pearl Harbor—but she said inelegantly, "Huh?"

"Any slob," Bonnie said, "can be nice to St. Francis of Assisi or Marlene Dietrich. It's how nice you are to the people you don't like that counts."

The room collapsed into normal with a diffuse, communal sigh, as the hostesses settled back in their chairs and started whispering to each other.

But the Hapsburg girl remained on her feet. Everybody eyed her with curiosity, and God's Angry Woman addressed her directly.

"If you don't like the Jews the way they are, what have you ever done to make them different, and why not?"

A few people in the front rows laughed, and somebody cried, "Hear! Hear!" But the Hapsburg girl paid no attention. She was staring incredulously at Bonnie. Then the girl in the next seat took her by the elbow and pulled her down, and Lucy went on with her talk.

When she finished, a few hostesses sprang up and endorsed the idea of sending the letter, but after that the meeting developed symptoms which would have brought an anticipatory gleam to the eye of an embalmer. When the Junior Hostesses are interested and enthusiastic, they remind you of corn popping. But this time they began scraping up meager little objections and shoving them forward tentatively, with the toe of the foot.

I won't rehearse the irrelevancies, comrade. We didn't know how to get the girls to sign, and they didn't know how to get out of signing. Not gracefully, anyway. The meeting dragged on till I began to think we'd all be found next season by the Forest Rangers, with our antlers locked. At one point a girl named

Muriel got up. The captains exchanged apprehensive glances. Muriel is the prettiest, most gently curved and generally adorable little blonde this side of Paradise. She is, in fact, an Anglo-Saxon houri. But intellectually, she got left way behind by the Seeing Eye dogs.

Muriel trustingly held her small, dimpled face up to Lucy.

"My father says the Jews are clannish."

She laid the statement in Lucy's lap like a child making her a present of a bright-colored pebble.

One of the captains said, "Oh, my good God!" in accents not redolent of admiration.

A Jewish Junior Hostess rose and smiled ruefully at Muriel.

"Nobody knows whether the Jews are clannish," she said. "Not even the Jews themselves."

Heads twisted in her direction. She's a markedly Jewish-looking girl, at least a decade older than Muriel.

"I have a friend—a Gentile—who lives in one of those beautiful, elm-shaded, New England villages. Some years ago she wanted me to rent a house there for the summer."

The Jewish girl moved her hand expressively.

"I told her what it would be like, but she didn't believe me. She tried to rent a house for me, and she found out."

At the back of the room, somebody coughed.

"This village goes back to Revolutionary times. If one had a criticism to make of it, it would be that the town is almost too much infatuated with its own Americanism. But my friend discovered that the village has a motto. It isn't carved in marble over the town hall. Only the Jews and the selectmen know it. The motto is, 'Keep the Jews out of the borough.' "

Muriel sat down abruptly.

"I can't rent a house in that village. I can't buy a house there. I can't even stay overnight at the town's only hotel. It doesn't take Jews."

The speaker straightened her shoulders.

"My brother has a house in one of the few small towns in that state where Jews are allowed to buy or rent property. So I go there in the summer. The selectmen in my friend's town look at each other triumphantly and say, 'You see. They're clannish. You let one in and they all come in.' "

There was a heavy silence.

"That's how it is," the Jewish hostess said, and sat down.

I looked fearfully at the Hapsburg girl, but she was sitting with her head bent, staring into her lap and not listening. I forgot about her when a composed, gray-eyed young woman I've always liked very much took the floor and said placidly that it was too bad a condition like that existed, and she was sorry about Mae Rabinowitz, but she thought sending the letter to Mrs. Sadler was wrong in principle. Such actions, she averred, only made anti-Semitism worse, because they made people more, instead of less, conscious of Jew and Gentile.

I said quickly that it was Mrs. Sadler, not any of us, who had made the original distinction between Jew and Gentile, but the point went unheeded. The Junior Hostesses who didn't want to sign the letter had been given a beautiful out, and they lost no time in embracing it. For disheartening endeavor in its purest form, Jeffie, I give you the job of trying to cope with the hush-hush theory about prejudice—the theory that if we all keep quiet and don't do anything, the Brownies will take it away overnight.

The gray-eyed girl said if we sent the letter to Mrs. Sadler, it would only make her more anti-Semitic than ever.

Impossible, retorted our side, because when it comes to anti-Semitic feeling, Mrs. Sadler is carrying a peak load right now.

Tempers were lost, and things grew decidedly astringent.

But the captains kept slogging away, and after a while it began to seem as if we were making a little progress. The difficulty was that at the rate we were going, we'd need another ten hours to make enough. In the midst of the travail, I glanced at Bonnie and was amazed to see that she looked entirely tranquil. She was gazing speculatively at the immobile, unlistening Hapsburg girl.

As if she sensed Bonnie's look, the Hapsburg girl jumped up.

"Talk, talk, talk!" she shouted, and though I shiv-

138

ered at the lunatic timbre of her voice, I couldn't help thinking that she had a point, all right.

"I care just as much about democracy as you do," she shrilled at Bonnie. "But I'm a realist and you're a sentimentalist. I happen to know there's such a thing as carrying democracy too far."

She was clutching her purse to her chest, and her handkerchief had been twisted into a string and was woven in and out through her fingers.

"You don't know now, but you'll see," she said wildly. "When the soldiers come back they aren't going to stand for it. The Jews and the niggers all over the place. When the soldiers come back, they're going to keep their guns. There's going to be a blood bath."

She turned and started pushing her way to the side aisle, where there was an exit. When she reached the aisle, she raked the Junior Hostesses with a hot, contemptuous stare.

"I'm sorry I ever joined this Canteen."

Her voice went up to a thin scream.

"There isn't a single pure American in it."

She surveyed the semi-circle of captains.

"As for *you*, you're all Jews yourselves. That's why you stick together."

"No," Bonnie said. "We're Mormons."

We all laughed—as much from gratitude, I think, as amusement—and the Hapsburg girl disappeared through the exit unnoticed.

139

Bonnie stood up.

"You see what Mae Rabinowitz is up against," she said, throwing the line away.

From my nerveless fingers she extracted the letter to Mrs. Sadler. She studied it for a minute, and then held it out to the Junior Hostesses.

"Who'll buy my violets?" she said.

We got 248 signatures, Jeff, out of a possible 300. That is, Bonnie got them. If Bonnie had had a carriage, the captains would certainly have taken the horses out and pulled it home by the shafts. While we were all swarming around her, I asked her how she could be so calm and gay about things that were so terrifying.

"You mean Bloody Mary? I used to nurse mental cases."

"Poor thing," she added. "She certainly was a break for us."

The Junior Hostess meeting was yesterday. Nothing noteworthy has happened today, except that Tom Garrett was supposed to come back. However, it's ten o'clock and he hasn't come in yet. I have made up my mind not to be embarrassed when I see him, and to greet him with utter composure and a series of light and graceful remarks. Unfortunately, my composure hasn't yet come off the assembly line, and the only remarks I have been able to think of wouldn't get by with King Kong. So it will be all right with me if he doesn't arrive until I've finished this and gone to bed. I'll go even further and say that if a fairy godmother were to give me three wishes, the first eight of them would be that I'd never have to see Tom Garrett again.

I've been thinking a good deal, in this blessedly peaceful interval while he's been away, of asking him to go warble his native wood-notes wild in somebody else's brother's room. But a realistic survey of the situation compels me to acknowledge that he won't go unless he chooses to, and since New York is already full of people who haven't where to lay their heads, he isn't likely to choose to. Besides which, Father would be difficult about it—a condition which strikes me as being not without irony. Father's never liked any of the men I liked—not that I liked them much myself, if you see what I mean—but when this vitamin-infested hulk steps in off the street and calls me shabby-genteel, Father gives him a welcome that makes the Rotarians look like morbid introverts.

I admit shamelessly (almost) that the reason I want Tom to go is because I can't manage him. Except for a couple of issues like Popsy's death-dealing pipe and your inconvenient and reasonless refusal to eat anything with chocolate in it, I've never found my father or my brother completely unmalleable. I could even put Philip through a hoop or two before he escaped me by lapsing into unconsciousness. But this bizarre and unregenerate alien doesn't play according to the rules. True, he adds elements of surprise and novelty to my perhaps too well-ordered existence, but the same could be said of having a tiger by the tail. And after all, Jeff, it's my house, isn't it? Well, Father's, perhaps, but I take care of it. And I'm entitled to live in it in peace if I want to, aren't I?

Not that I intend to cross swords with our lodger about his going, having learned from experience that all I'd get out of that would be the exercise. I'm going to be a sly-boots. I'm going to have a one-woman underground movement . . .

There goes a key in the lock.

It was only Father, coming back from the Ration Board. But I might as well go to bed and finish this in the morning. I'm scared.

March 16th

My dear Geoffrey,

Do you think it was quite, quite wise to accept two stripes from the U. S. Army? Remember what Aunt Julie always says—only flowers and candy, otherwise people might get the wrong idea.

But seriously, Jeffie, how swell! You really are a delightful and accomplished gent, aren't you? The occasion seemed of sufficient moment to call up Father at the office and tell him.

"The rank is but the guinea stamp," he said quickly, with an air of utterly unconvincing deprecation.

You're putting the Progenitor to a lot of trouble, Jeff. He's finding it increasingly difficult to conceal his pride in you under the air of gruff detachment which he thinks is What The Well-Repressed Man Will Wear.

Me, I'm not troubled by any notions of being either gruff or detached. I'm just going to sit down and embroider "Habeas Corporal" on all my handkerchiefs.

Your letter, coming today, was even more than usually welcome. I suppose it's what is technically known as a pretty kettle of fish when the boys in service have to cheer up the folks at home, but today is certainly one of our less palatable segments of eternity. The warm weather yesterday turned out to be a false front. Today it is winter again and nothing is left of the spring but a bouncing, eight-pound cold I caught from going around with my coat open. Also, Tom Garrett hasn't come back. His arrivals are always somewhat inexact, but he told Father he'd be back by yesterday at the latest, and he's never been later than "at the latest" before. I suppose it could be engine trouble or bad weather. If anything has happened to him, I'm going to feel like a murderess.

"Who killed Cock Robin?"

"I," said the Sparrow,

"With the merest touch of wishful thinking."

I won't mail this till tomorrow. Perhaps by then I'll be able to report that he's back.

In the meantime, darling, it's wonderful about the stripes. I love to think of you wearing them, and strenuously cultivating the habit of ordering people around.

No Tom.

I'll wait another day before I put this in the mail.

Father drummed on the table all through breakfast this morning, until I finally said in shrewish tones that if he wanted to act out "The Spirit of '76," would he please wait till he got the two other guys?

Kinda purty, ain't it?

This has been an unnerving day, and I can remember feeling better just after having been trodden out by the bare feet of the peasants. For instance. This morning I was enjoying a five-minute respite (my first, and probably due to sheer exhaustion) from feeling guilty and worried about Tom. I was washing the breakfast dishes, while a man addressed me compellingly over the radio.

"Folks," he said, "what would you do if the man you loved were accused of being a criminal? Would you stand by him, as lovely Maggie Mayo did? . . ."

I decided I wouldn't, because if *I* loved him, he'd probably really *be* a criminal. I dried the Silex and turned around to put it on the shelf. Tom was standing in the kitchen door, with his arm in a sling. I dropped the Silex, and it fell on the floor and broke.

"Lady," Tom said, "I certainly hope you're planning to marry a glass blower."

My knees evaporated.

144

"I didn't mean to startle you," he apologized. "I called, but I guess you didn't hear on account of the radio."

I sat down on the kitchen stool. Thoroughly. Of the next few moments, it is my recollection that I gave a rather distinguished portrayal of mental deficiency. When my lips felt dry, I realized I'd been improving the shining hour by letting my mouth hang open.

"Then you didn't get killed?"

Even to my fond and prejudiced ear, the remark sounded unintelligent.

Tom smiled faintly.

"Close, but no cigar."

He sagged against the door jamb and rubbed his eyes with the back of his free hand.

"I'm tired. Could you fix me some breakfast?"

Fixing breakfast is a province where I may reasonably claim to be on home ground. By the time I had swept up the Silex and activated my Lares and Penates, I began to feel less shaken. I was vastly curious about what had happened to Tom's arm, but he had gone into the living room and stretched out on the sofa. Besides, my research work with you and Father has taught me never to ask questions of a hungry male. The answers are seldom imbued with that Old World courtliness to which I am so partial.

But the advent of food did not, apparently, make Tom feel that he wanted to live in a house by the side of the road and be a friend to man. He ate in a preoccupied way and said briefly that starting back, he had crashed on the take-off; that he had had no sleep; and that he was going to bed. I asked what had happened to his arm and he gave me a sour look and said, "Nothing." Wearing a sling on a sound arm seemed to me a new departure in mortifying the flesh, but I didn't say so. Tom went to bed and I telephoned Father and told him Hell's Angel had returned.

Tom's breakfast having delayed me, I spent the rest of the day racing against time because I had to be at the Canteen early. After the Junior Hostess meeting, the captains agreed to take turns carrying Mrs. Sadler's letter around the Canteen to get signatures from the girls who hadn't been at the meeting. Mine was the last stint, and I found that signing the letter had developed the proportions of a vogue. Everybody was talking about it, and the Junior Hostesses were more agreeably stimulated than they've been at any time since the snood came back. My spirits, as the fellow says, soared.

It was about nine o'clock when I saw Mr. Richards bearing down on me, and I didn't need my litmus paper and my Chemcraft set to discern that he was in a towering rage. Panic turned me into a block of ice. Mr. Richards halted in front of me and tried to snatch the letter from my hand. Since that extremity was paralyzed in a viselike grip, and I couldn't have opened it if I'd wanted to, the result of this gesture was to tilt me forward till I nearly made a three-point landing on the seigneurial stomach. Mr. Richards let go of the letter and pushed me back, from which vantage point he gave me a look that would have raised blisters on a Black Widow spider.

"You'll hear more of this," he said viciously, and walked off.

My heart finally concluding that there wasn't really room for it among my tonsils, I peered cautiously around; but the incident had happened so quickly that nobody, it seemed, noticed it. I got my hat and coat and took the letter to the Post Office. When it was safely in the mail, I came home. If Tom had recovered his joie de vivre and wanted to make cheering utterances about the rencontre, I was not prepared to object. But he was out. I called Bonnie and Lucy, and they both said they didn't see what Mr. Richards could do. He couldn't ask most of the Junior Hostesses to resign, because then he wouldn't have any Canteen. He might ask all the captains to resign, but it would be hard to replace them. The job being full of tedious detail and not uniformly rewarding, people don't lust after it.

Lucy and Bonnie decided there was nothing to worry about, but I dunno . . . They didn't see Mr. Richards, and I did. Mr. R. has heard that the meek shall inherit the earth, but he figures there are quicker ways to get your hands on it. If he doesn't do anything, it won't be for lack of trying.

Should you not hear from me, you may conclude that Mr. Richards has had me razed to the ground and planted with salt, like Carthage.

Love,
Gretchen

147

Dear Bro.,

Tell me not, in mournful numbers, that you can't get a three-day pass. Shucks! But on second thought, un-Shucks! Because Father and I decided we wouldn't repine, it being really much harder on you than on us. We can get drunk or eat lotus to take the edge off the disappointment, whereas you're limited to whatever consolation you can get out of saying "Kismet" or "C'est la guerre" or "Well, that's show business." Not that I entirely blame your C.O. If I had a brand-new corporal with a deadly aim, I wouldn't let him out of my sight for a minute, either. So we're keeping stiff upper lips (though I don't know how they'd look if we took the cardboard out from under them). And Father said, when he read your letter, "Well, that means the war will be over three days sooner."

The snapshot is wonderful, and tongue cannot tell how we devoured it. How much weight have you put on? However much it is, it was just what you needed to keep your book larnin' from showing. It seemed queer to see your familiar old face jutting out of a uniform, but you certainly look nifty in your plumage. Were you really as happy as you seemed to be, when the camera caught you? Or were you just grinning because our family, when chided for not leaving its uncut emeralds on the coffee table, always points to Geoffrey's teeth and says, "These are our jewels"?

But seriously, we are awfully thankful to have the picture. It makes us feel much more in touch with you.

I'm going to take it up to Janie's tomorrow. Janie has been trying loyally to keep your memory green in Deborah's mind, but somewhere along the way she apparently made a serious blunder, because Deborah has got you inextricably mixed up with the Easter Bunny. Uncle Jeff, she thinks, is the one whose head lifts off to reveal a cache of jelly beans. This has not, I may say, prejudiced her against you. Quite the reverse. Her main enthusiasm, though, is still her old man. Having observed that Bill always takes a book to the bathroom with him after breakfast, she now refuses to sit on her potty unless she has a book, too. "Daddy does," she remarks, fingering the volume and looking up at you with her little, teeny, big blue eyes. I asked Bill how he liked this last full measure of devotion, and he looked rather confused and mumbled that if she didn't stop, he was going to send her back to Lord & Taylor.

That's all the news for the present, except that Tom Garrett must have had a really bad crash, because he has drawn into his shell and nothing sticks out except an occasional terse "Good morning" or "Good night." He spends a good deal of time in his room, with the door closed, and when he does emerge, I tiptoe silently around him in wide circles. This would be the happiest arrangement I've ever had with him, except that I think if he's been through a little bit of all wrong, he'd be better off to talk about it. But when I said as much to Father, he said, "Leave him alone." So I do, though it doesn't sit well with the Flossie Nightingale streak in me.

Nothing has happened about the letter to Mrs. Sadler. She and Mr. Richards frequent the Canteen as usual, looking like Mr. and Mrs. Loch Ness Monster, but as they never have the air of people who have just come to the prize in the bottom of the Crackerjack box, nothing can be inferred from this. Mrs. Richards, perhaps, flutters a little more than usual. There is a Mrs. Richards, though I don't know whether I've ever mentioned her before. She is a large woman, and her figure is a living monument to the tensile strength of pink brocade; but I have the impression that she has lived in a state of chronic fright ever since she turned away from the altar with her grim bridegroom twenty-five years ago. Whenever anything happens to upset her, which is every three minutes, she clasps her hands and says helplessly to Mr. R., "Oh, *William* . . .!" Mr. Richards treats her with elaborate, old-fashioned courtesy which doesn't serve—to a female observer, anyway—to hide his contempt for her. I myself would rather be hit in the face than addressed as "My dear" in the tone Mr. Richards reserves for his helpmeet, but I guess Mrs. Richards had her choice and selected "My dear."

If I don't run the vacuum over the living room rug right this minute, some nearsighted bystander is going to mistake it for the beach after a storm. So this is all for now. I'll write again in a few days—unless the Iron Twain have me picked up for impersonating an officer.

Love,
Gretchen

Treasured Dogface:

Though I keep telling the real-estate company that our house, like the projected one at Innisfree, is of clay and wattles made, I cannot truthfully add that peace comes dropping slow. I wish it did.

Yesterday afternoon I bought, among other comestibles, a handsome and shapely beef tongue. In the act of decanting it into the icebox, I had a sudden impulse—obedient to which, I put the tongue on Tom's dresser and pinned a little note to it saying, "This is to help you lick your wounds." By the time I finished putting away the groceries, I had decided it was a pretty silly thing to do; but just as I set out to retrieve the viand, Tom came in. He went to his room without speaking to me, but in a moment I heard him snort and laugh ha-Ha.

"Bless your heart," he said, coming into the kitchen.

He put the tongue on the table and his face sobered.

"My navigator was killed."

Tightening his lips, he added, "And I have to sit around on my tail on account of this damned arm."

Isn't it funny, Jeff, how fluently sympathetic you can be with people you privately consider are making

151

a fuss over nothing? But when you really want to lighten someone's burden, you just stand there like a goop. No nobler consolation occurred to me than to ask Tom if he'd have some beer. He would. We took it into the living room and had a feast of reason and a flow of soul, until he said he had to get out to the airport.

At the front door, he turned back and asked if I'd be here tomorrow night (that's tonight).

I said I would.

"Will Greene is in town on a furlough. May I bring him around for a drink?"

(Will Greene—I think I've told you—is the Negro newspaperman who once saved Tom's life.)

I started to say, "Why, yes, of course," but I was halted by an uninvigorating thought. To wit: Father. I've had my Negro Junior Hostesses at the house whenever I had any occasion to, but I've never had a Negro man here. There's a Canteen rule that you mustn't make dates with servicemen you meet there, and it is broken less frequently than you might think. By the time a person has finished a long evening dancing with the military, her desire to soak her feet is little short of obsessive. Some instinct told me that Father, who peers with equal inattentiveness at white and Negro Junior Hostesses, was going to regard a Negro soldier— to use an ill-chosen phrase—as a horse of another color.

"Well," I said slowly, "somebody will have to break it to Father. He'll be here tomorrow night."

"Somebody will, indeed," Tom answered, with the

152

excessive cheerfulness that heralds all his most un-settling ideas.

The ensuing argument was concluded when Tom said, "I'll tell you what. You tackle him first, and then if you don't get anywhere, I'll take him on."

I slammed the beer glasses down on the tray.

"There's been only one thing in my life that I've always regretted," I said angrily.

"What's that?"

"I neglected to get run over at the age of four."

Tom laughed and went out.

Father was in a mellow and benevolent mood at dinner I made three false starts about bringing up the subject of Will Greene's coming and finally gave it up, concluding that I owed it to my digestive juices to wait till I'd finished the dishes. I washed all the canisters and the breadbox, as well as the dishes, hoping that Father would fall asleep or decide to go up to Janie's; but he stayed awake and read the paper and puffed away contentedly at Germany's Secret Weapon.

When there was no longer any postponing it, I strolled into the living room—if it can be called strolling when your knees are waving like grain in the wind.

"Tom Garrett wants to bring a soldier here to-morrow night," I commented feebly.

"All right."

Father didn't look up from the paper.

"The soldier is a Negro," I blurted out.

"All right."

I looked at him.

153

He put down his pipe and the paper.

"*What?*"

"You heard me," I quavered. "Tom wants to bring a Negro soldier here tomorrow night."

Father smiled pleasantly.

"Garrett wouldn't do that."

"Yes, he would."

"Tell him he can't, then," Father said irritably, and went back to the paper.

"But he can."

I was alarmed to notice that my voice was beginning to sound like the Hapsburg girl's.

"I told him he could."

Father laid down the paper. For keeps.

"Now that's enough of that," he roared.

He got up and paced back and forth in front of the fireplace. More quietly, he said, "I haven't said anything about it, but I've never liked this work you do at the Canteen. For just this reason."

He paused and kicked at the fire screen.

"It isn't that I have anything against Negroes. I haven't. The women are fine."

He began to pace again, but stopped to turn on me.

"Big black bucks *look* at you."

I flared up.

"Oh, they do, do they? Well, if you want to know, big white bucks *look* at me, too. Also little white bucks. If you don't want me to be *looked* at, why don't you keep me indoors?"

I started to cry. In spades, and in glorious Technicolor.

154

"Why don't you have all my teeth pulled, too, while you're at it?"

I sank to the sofa and buried my head in the pillows. But I yanked it up again immediately and said, "I take care of this house, and I ought to be able to have anybody here I want to."

Father collapsed into the red chair.

"Oh, my goodness!" he moaned. "Oh, my *goodness!*"

I surfaced again.

"And furthermore, if I can't have him here, then I'm going to get a war job and you can take care of your own darn house."

Father was appalled. Except for the day you went to the Army, when he felt like crying himself, Popsy hasn't seen me weep since I came home from Philip's house—if a domicile for which Father was so largely the breadwinner could, strictly speaking, be described as Philip's.

"You don't mean it," he said. "You don't know what you're saying."

I kept on crying, because I was so terrified and miserable, but after a while I began to speculate on whether the tears were going to spot the sofa pillows. How long I could hold out without blowing my nose was another subject for reflection, but luckily, groping down behind the seat cushion, I found an old piece of Kleenex. (I wouldn't tell this to anybody but you, as it is a damaging reflection on the extent of my spring cleaning.)

"It's impossible," Father said. "You're only a woman. You don't understand."

I looked up and saw that he had his elbows on his knees and was propping up his forehead with his hands. I went and sat on the floor in front of him.

"Please let me have him here."

He took out his handkerchief and handed it to me, which was a good thing, as the Kleenex had been swept out to sea.

"Look," I began . . .

We talked for an hour, Jeff, and Father's imperviousness to reason was by way of being a virtuoso performance. After an infinity of broken field running, bobbing and weaving, and other evasive action that he must have learned from a stomach dancer, he concluded by saying that this soldier was probably a sex maniac, or at best a marijuana addict.

"He's a friend of Tom's," I said.

Father put her hard aport. When I do things like having this Negro soldier at the house, he said, it just makes a certain number of Americans start talking about white supremacy.

My intuition has always made me distrust this argument, but Tom was the one who put his finger on the flaw in it. There's nothing you can do about the race problem, Tom says, that's safe. We've let it go too long for that. The only choice we have left is between perilous courses that are democratic and perilous courses that aren't democratic.

"I concede your point," I said to Father. "If I have this soldier here, it makes a certain number of Americans start talking about white supremacy. But that isn't all."

156

"Indeed."

"It also makes a certain number of colored Americans feel that white people really do know how to play fair. It makes them want to do everything they can, from their side, to help resolve the dilemma."

Father, unfortunately, wasn't listening.

"Suppose I say you can't have this soldier here?"

I scrambled to my feet.

"I meant what I said. If he can't come here, I'm going to get a job. I won't keep house for you any more."

I've never believed that people turn white, as per the less pretentious forms of literature, but they do. Father did. There was a long, exquisitely painful silence. I was trembling from head to foot.

"All right," Father said at length, speaking with thinned lips. "He can come."

He got up and went to his room and shut the door.

Oh, Jeffie, it was awful! He looked so stricken and haggard I thought my heart would break. It seemed as if I couldn't bear it not to run after him and say, "Never mind, darling, forget it. Let it go."

But I didn't. I just stood there.

Briefly, the rest of the night warn't a fit one for man nor beast. I must have gotten some sleep, because I didn't hear Tom come in, but it seemed as if I were awake all night. One minute I would think of Father's ashy, ruined face—my handiwork!—and the next I thought of all the innocent people who have been exploited and beaten up and dishonored because of the scientifically untenable theory that big black bucks *look* at you.

Breakfast was ghastly. Father looked ten years older and wouldn't touch anything but coffee. When it became apparent that he wasn't going to speak to me, I summoned the lightest inflection I could muster (which wasn't very light) and said tentatively, "I could not love thee, dear, so much, loved I not honor more."

Father put down his napkin and surveyed me with the level gaze of unqualified hatred.

"You've got your own way. Isn't that enough?"

I tried to say "No," but I couldn't talk, so I only shook my head.

Father smiled grimly.

After he left, I started in with the hewing of wood and drawing of water. When Tom came down the hall, on his way out, I was in the living room with an oil mop as my only visible means of support. Tom looked in, and after what seemed a considerable lapse of time, asked softly, "Well?"

"It's all right."

I detached myself from the mop long enough to jab it under the nearest chair.

He came in and put his hand on my shoulder.

"That's the stuff to give the troops," he said, in a gentle voice, and after squeezing my arm sympathetically, he went out.

So there it is, Jeff. One more such victory and I am ruined. What is giving me a seagoing nervous breakdown is that I felt more as if I were talking to a Storm

Trooper than to my once-doting Pa. I expected a fuss about Will Greene, because I knew the idea would startle Father and he hates to have his ivory tower invaded. But I can't understand the intensity of his resistance. He's always been a just and generous man, in his high-handed way, and from time immemorial, he's thought more of me than he does of his right hand. I don't want to stump the Expert, but why is he acting like this? If it makes sense to you, please lead, Kindly Light, amid the encircling gloom.

I've renewed your aging magazine subscriptions, and yesterday I sent you a couple of Pocket Books which I noticed when I was in the drugstore and which seemed to be of a diverting and healthily unedifying nature. The one bright spot in the present low-pressure area is that I've thought up a wondrous birthday gift for you. You may start right in licking your chops. But I must stop instantly, because I find I'm horribly tempted to break down and tell you what it is.

Affectionately,
Gretchen

March 26th

Dear Bro.,

It's a weary, weary world we're livin' in th' noo, and in case you're inclined to dispute the point, I have documentary evidence. This morning Lucy and Bonnie and I got letters from the Canteen Governing Board. The letters said it had come to the Board's attention that we were causing a disturbance in the Canteen and they thought that, in the best interest of the war effort, we had better resign. We wrote a joint letter in reply, asking whether they didn't think our long service at the Canteen entitled us to a more detailed explanation.

This is all for now. I have to get out my First Aid handbook and look up the section on What To Do Till The Tumbrel Comes.

Hastily,

G.

P.S. It really hurts, though. We didn't refrain from putting some of our heart's blood into that place, and it's sharper than a serpent's tooth to be asked to leave. Under a shadow.

P.P.S. Tom brought Will Greene to the house last night. (Father went up to Janie's.) Will is tall and medium brown, with a haughty face, like a Pharaoh's —aquiline nose and sharply modeled lips—but upon acquaintance he turned out to be mild to the point of insipidity. He and I tried discussing books, but we didn't seem to have read very many of the same ones, and I thought him distressingly flaccid and uncritical about several little opera that I wouldn't hesitate to describe as saccharine. Before I worked at the Canteen, I would have found it hard to believe that anyone so sentimental could also be so handy with a burning airplane, but one thing you learn at our 59th Street palais de danse is that a man can be a hero and be a crashing bore, too. (And unless you're willing to take him both ways, it's kinder to ignore him altogether.)

Belles-lettres having been given Christian burial, Tom and Will plunged into one of those cryptic, enthusiastic, masculine conversations to which the women of America owe some of their best ideas for doing over the living room and fixing last year's hat to seem less, as the dictionary so trenchantly puts it, (Obs.). Tom and Will talked mostly about flying and about the Army, and though I was inattentive, I could see that Tom's fondness for Will doesn't come from his great indebtedness. Rather, it is one of those perverse attachments men sometimes have for other men with whom they appear to have nothing in common—like your inexplicable affection for Jerry Mayhew. (Yes, darling, I know Jerry Mayhew has a heart of gold. But I can't talk to him through a stethoscope.)

I guess I'm being mean, aren't I? Forgive me, feller. My nervous system wasn't designed for championing underdogs. But then, whose was?

I must say for Will that, like so many Negroes, he is courteous right to the bone. I was a little ashamed when he said good-by, because his leave-taking made me feel as if I'd been a much better hostess than I actually was.

After Will had gone, I told Tom about the scene with Father last night. Tom said I must remember that it has been a great shock for Father. It hasn't been poppy and mandragora for me, to discover that my sensitive, humorous, intelligent parent has such a wide streak of passionate unreason, but I let the point go.

"I'll remember." I promised. "Father will see to that."

I pointed to the clock.

"Bill and Janie never stay up this late. Father's gone to a movie, so as to give me plenty of time to imagine him jumping off a bridge."

"Put a spike in his wheel," Tom suggested. "Imagine him falling under a taxi, instead."

This started out to be just a little whiff of postscript, and it has reached proportions which suggest that the shrimp is not going to be cooked in time for dinner.

Without further ado,

Affectionately,

Gretchen

P.S. to the P.P.S. As predicted by Tom, Father got home at two o'clock, unabrased and uncontused.

March 27th

Dear Jeff,

Janie has just called me. She says she can't understand how I could be so cruel to Father. She says she never wants to see me again, and she doesn't propose to let Deborah get contaminated by associating with me.

"It would be bad enough," she said, "if it were a

white man, but a coal-black darky who probably stole the spoons . . ."

"He isn't coal-black and he didn't . . . ," I began, but Janie had hung up.

Reeling is the word for Gretchen. I can't believe it of Father, Jeffie. I can't believe he went and talked to Janie. He knows perfectly well that in our household, appealing to Janie has always been considered an off-side play. I suppose it's what is called a compensation mechanism. I mean, the way Janie—perhaps to make up for her otherwise almost excessive serenity—hangs on to her infrequent grudges for years. Even after she's forgotten what they came from. But it doesn't matter what it is. What matters is that it's quite in the cards for me not to see Deborah again till she's halfway grown up. And Father knows that.

Golly!

He stoops to conquer, doesn't he?

But he hasn't been very clever about it. Some people can work it so that they get thirty pieces of silver, besides the emotional satisfaction.

At first I wasn't going to write you about this, not wishing to impair your morale with a story of ructions at home. But then I realized that you'll probably get a communication from Janie which will not be remarkable for the closeness of its reasoning. So I thought I'd better let you know that though the home front is neither mirthful nor variegated, I haven't yet found it so dull that I have to resort to patricide to pep things up.

163

Anyway, you will know how to interpret Janie.

I'll write again when I'm more composed. Deborah . . . oh, God!

Love,
G.

Bewitching Corporal:

The newspapers adjure me almost daily to keep my letters to you cheerful, so I'm rather conscience-stricken about my recent lapse from jollity. However, if my epistles have been of an unsettling nature, I can now promise you what the advertisements describe as immediate relief. From here in, my correspondence is going to be as pellucid as the Twenty-third Psalm—the reason being that I've reached a point where I have nobody left to alienate.

I went into the estrangement business in quite a small way. Just the superintendent and the real-estate company were all I had to start with. But by clean living and not opening charge accounts, I managed to extend it to include Father and Janie. It wasn't until this morning, though, that I made the final acquisition. This morning Bonnie and Lucy and I got another letter from the Governing Board. The Board said they thought it only right to tell us that, in the event of our being unwise enough to try to return to the Canteen, we would be refused admission.

Chin down was the way I took this blow. Showing

164

the letter to Tom, I paid a somewhat belated tribute to the fruitful stratagem of leaving well enough alone.

"Before we do-gooders started to meddle," I said, "there was some doubt in Mrs. Sadler's mind, and in other people's minds, as to just how far she could go with her unlovely vagaries. But not any more—thanks to us. We cleared it all up. It's now definitely established that the old tarantula can have a free hand with her pogroms, and no questions asked."

Tom objected.

"You're taking a morbid view of it. Not to say melodramatic."

"No, I'm not. Lucy and Bonnie and I will disappear from the Canteen. Nobody will know the exact circumstances, but everybody will observe that if you don't want to be liquidated, you'd better not tamper with Mrs. Sadler's prejudices. We've done just the opposite of what we meant to do. Instead of weakening her hold, we've strengthened it."

"When it comes to nobody's knowing the exact circumstances of your leaving," Tom said, "I can think of a way to obviate that."

The outcome of this remark was that Bonnie and Lucy and I wrote a letter which—after it has been mimeographed—we're going to send to all the people who work at the Canteen. Not just the Junior Hostesses, but the Seniors, too, and the people who work in the kitchen, the office and the checkroom—as well as the plumber, the electrician and the man who mops the floor. In the letter, we described the Rabinowitz affair from the very beginning, and wound up by including our recent correspondence with the Governing Board. To make the letter perfectly clear and yet not have it too long was a job which took most of the afternoon, and I couldn't help reflecting sadly that it's an ill wind, etc. Now that I have been unfrocked by the Governing Board, I'll have time to finish up the spring cleaning. How disheveled this apartment has gotten, while I've been laboring in other vineyards, is a thing I could discuss at length, only I know you'd consider it an unvital statistic.

Bonnie is stony broke, owing to a careless habit of educating her nephews, so Lucy and I are going to pay for the mimeographing. I'm using the doubloons which my guardian angel—before they declared him 1-A—prevented me from spending on a new hat. Lucy and I swallowed hard when we found out how much the job is going to cost, but the woman who seemed to be in charge of the place where they do it was so much impressed by our letter that she's going to cut the stencil herself, tonight, so that we can have the copies tomorrow, and she's going to do the stapling free. How warmed and fortified we were by this gesture, Bro., I can't tell you. We practically promised the woman to name our children after her. Logical behavior—we are discovering without pleasure—is the shortest cut to being lonely.

Unfortunately, the mimeograph woman isn't the Governing Board—though it would certainly have been an ideal arrangement if she were—and Bonnie

166

and Lucy and I are unhappily aware that the suicide squad was more aptly named than we had thought. For a few days after we send out the letter, there will be a storm of talk around the Canteen; but all the Board has to do is sit tight and it will blow over and be forgotten. Tom, who always seems to be cheerful in the wrong places, says gaily that we're going down fighting. That, however, is one of those trick remarks men make to whip themselves up to a pitch of unwarranted optimism. Women, being more practical, do not fail to note that though it may be true that we're fighting, it's equally true that we're going down.

Between the Canteen, and the fact that Father won't speak to me unless it's absolutely necessary, I am oppressed by a feeling that in any well-organized competition for popular affection, I would come in for a photo finish with the Dust Bowl.

Heigh-ho.

Whom the Lord loveth, He chasteneth. But I can't help wishing that somebody would give Him a couple of new telephone numbers.

I stopped in at the lab last week to take your messages to Roentzen and show the snapshot to The Girls You Left Behind You. Roentzen looks very tired and says you must have done the work of three men, but wants me to tell you he'll make out. I suspect the poor wight is not as good an organizer as you.

The Girls gobbled up your picture. At least, Mlles. Adelman and Stafford chorused that you look simply *darling* in your uniform and you still have your wonderful smile, while Miss Ellsworth acquiesced in a manner culled from the best texts on Office Practice. But you are one soldier, old boy, who cannot complain that the stay-at-homes don't appreciate his hardships. Miss Ellsworth is in agony at the idea of your shining your own shoes and sewing on your own buttons. Much as she admires your Commander in Chief, she is afraid he doesn't know an exquisite amalgam of Percy Bysshe Shelley and young Dr. Kildare when he sees it.

The Misses Adelman and Stafford are also dubious about the Young Marster's doing his own valeting, but they put it more on the ground that you must be fantastically inept. I said I thought steps had been taken to assure your competence in that direction, and this gave them a fit of the giggles. They are writing you a poem, which you will probably receive ere long. (Every time they're ready to write "Finis," they think of another verse.) The poem started out to be a nostalgic evaluation of the absent hero, but when they got to contemplating your personal idiosyncrasies . . .

However, I mustn't spoil it for you.

A glance at the clock confirms my impression that I can only be on time at the hairdresser's by running every step of the way. So with the hastiest of adieus, and a silent prayer that I won't be flung back on *True Confessions* because the other customers have got all the movie magazines, I'm off.

Love,
Gretchen

Dear Jeff,

I never thought to see the day when I would sit down and write to anyone—even the world's leading brother—before washing the breakfast dishes. But that is what I am doing now, so uneven has the tenor of my ways become. I'm really in a cul-de-sac this time, Jeffie. Deader ends may have been devised than the one now tenanted by your sister Gretchen, but it would take a bit of proving. An illimitable and unprecedented listlessness has selected me for its field of operations, so that even writing to you involves an unnerving expenditure of energy. But it seemed a better idea than sitting still and drowning in melancholia. And I am fully resolved to be broken on the wheel before I will touch those dishes.

I suppose I'd better begin at the beginning.

Yesterday afternoon Bonnie and Lucy and I got our letter back from the mimeographing place, and last night Lucy went to the Canteen office and took the files, so that we'd have the addresses for the envelopes. Lucy being—or, more correctly, having been—a department head at the Canteen, she has a key to the office. A generous and inspired architect equipped the office with a back door, and it can be reached without going through the Canteen. I don't know whether it was ethical for us to take the files, but since Bonnie and Lucy were part of the small group which typed and alphabetized them in the first place, we concluded they might be said to have a claim on them.

Besides, a skirmish with the Iron Twain demands a variety of weapons, but the Boy Scout Oath is not one of them.

We each took a third of the envelopes to address. The events of the past few days have not made me feel as if I were living on a health farm, and by the time I had endured a wordless dinner with Father, cleaned up the kitchen, put the laundry together, and ironed some handkerchiefs for my mute, inglorious forebear, I was so tired I needed a trellis to keep me upright. But the files had to be back in the office by nine o'clock this morning, so there was no postponing the dreary little chore. Father departed for some unspecified destination and I started in on the envelopes. The job did not go swimmingly. I kept making mistakes, and I was haunted by a notion that the errors I caught were only about a third of the ones I made and that most of the letters would never reach the people they were meant for. By the time Tom came in, I was feeling hopeless, defeated, and monumentally ill-used. Not, in a word, amenable to reason.

"I-come-from-haunts-of-coot-and-hern-I-make-a-sudden-sally," Tom said, throwing his newspaper on the table from across the room. "How's the poor little motherless child?"

"Fatherless, too," I supplemented disagreeably. "Thanks to your benign intervention."

I suppose, considering that he was the last friend I had in the world, a modicum of tolerance, forbearance and self-restraint was in order. But I was under sway of the recollection that if Tom hadn't persuaded me to take up the cudgels for Mae Rabinowitz, I'd still be at the Canteen; and if he hadn't asked to bring Will Greene to the house, I'd still be seeing Deborah.

Tom had been about to sit down, but instead he came over and picked up the top envelope on the pile. It read as follows:

```
Kiss Angela Li/yons

335 West ＳＳ ＳＭＸＸ ＸＸ 56 Sr

N.
    Y.
        Cuty
```

"Why don't you go to bed?" he asked. "You can set the alarm for five o'clock and finish these in the morning."

"No."

"I wish I knew how to type. I'd do them for you myself."

"All you know how to do," I remarked bitterly, "is maneuver people into spots that would be considered unenviable by the Lost Battalion."

Tom glanced at me speculatively.

"The paterfamilias still sulking in his tent?"

I put another envelope into the typewriter.

"Be patient with him," Tom said. "He's unemployed."

I evinced no interest in this provocative statement, but Tom went ahead anyway.

"For twenty-six years, your father has been doing all your thinking for you. Now you're doing it for yourself, and he's out of a job. It's only natural for him to resent it."

"Do you mind not talking? I have work to do."

Tom smiled impenitently.

"I hoped I could cheer, if not inebriate. But I see I'm not in favor with Madame la Duchesse this evening."

I stood up from the typewriter.

"You're not in favor any evening. All my life I've disliked . . ."

"Yes?"

"Squatty little men," I said sweetly, "whose hair is beginning to get thin on top."

Tom sighed.

"Oh, Lord. So we're back to that again!"

"How much longer," he added, "do you think I'm going to keep on listening to that rot?"

"I couldn't possibly say. It's not a question I've ever asked myself."

Tom crossed the room and stood in front of me. Seeing him directly before me, I had to admit that he is much bigger than, perhaps, I have led you to believe; but I was not in the mood to make concessions.

"If you'd like to know the truth," I said, "I think you're physically repulsive."

As an aid to sluggish circulation, there is a good deal to be said for the feeling of having gone too far. For a minute, I thought Tom was going to hit me; but he conquered his reflexes, stepped back, put his hands in his pockets, and smiled.

"Since I'm not making any passes at you," he said smoothly, "aren't your sentiments more or less academic?"

He turned and went to his room.

I set my alarm for five o'clock. I had reached the saturation point.

The two spaces, Tovarisch, represent an interval of deliberation on whether or not to send this letter. It arrives, I notice on rereading, at no more exhilarating conclusion than that your communicant is not much of a hand for feathering her nest.

Well, I'll decide later.

I got up at five o'clock—an unrefreshing activity, if ever I saw one—and finished the envelopes. Lucy is housebound with sinus and Bonnie goes to work with the rosy-fingered dawn, so I undertook to collect their files and envelopes and get the files back to the Canteen office before it opened. I was so depressed I could hardly persuade my feet to arrange themselves in the customary sequences; but it didn't seem fair to penalize Bonnie and Lucy for my own lavish misdeeds, so as soon as Father's breakfast was on the table, I went out. (The one savory moment of the whole grim morning was when Father almost burned out a bearing trying not to ask me where I was going at that time of day.) I've just gotten back. Tom and Father have both gone, and I have to put the letters into their envelopes and mail them, but that can wait.

Oh, Jeff, I'm really shattered! It wasn't the sort of remark for which there is any conceivable apology.

173

You can't just drift up to a person and say lightly, "Don't mind me, neighbor—I learned my drawing room manners from the Ku Klux Klan." I don't know what to do. Not, actually, that there *is* anything to do—except wait till somebody comes along and induces me to step off a cliff, like the Gadarene swine. Pending that happy event, the atmosphere in this household is probably not going to put anybody in mind of waiting on the levee for the Robert E. Lee. I literally cower when I think of

Later

Oh, Jeff! Oh, golly! I don't know how to tell you! While I was deciding, reluctantly, that you have plenty of oi-weh and wurra wurra chez vous and I mustn't send you this letter, the phone rang. A secretary, upon being assured that I was I, said Mr. Richards wanted to talk to me.

Mr. Richards came on the wire as if he had been experiencing some difficulty in staying off it.

"*What . . . do you . . . think . . . you're . . . doing?*" he said.

For a moment I was too much surprised to have any sensations at all, and then I began to be puzzled. The envelopes were on my dresser, the files were back in the Canteen office, the letters were in our living room, and nobody had seen them except the woman in the mimeographing place. Mr. Richards couldn't possibly know about them yet.

I made a querying noise.

Mr. Richards repeated the question—upon which, a miracle happened. Nothing in Mr. R.'s inflection suggested that he had been working out on lullabies, but for the first time since I've been at the Canteen, I wasn't afraid of him. I just didn't have any emotion left, and the absence of it, where Mr. Richards was concerned, was such a delightful experience that for a minute I almost considered Tom and Deborah and the Canteen well lost.

"What am I doing?" I said amiably. "I'm trying to light a cigarette with one hand. What are *you* doing?"

There was a long pause. Mr. Richards is not accustomed to being addressed with airy insouciance by me.

At length, however, he appeared to get adjusted to it, and with an only slightly strained calm, he told me the story. When Bonnie left our house yesterday, she took one of the letters with her. For her memory book, she said. On her way home, she encountered one of her Junior Hostesses, with whom she had a bite to eat and to whom, for some reason, she gave her copy of the letter. This Junior Hostess is conspicuously free from warts, wens, enlarged pores and other infirmities that keep a damsel from getting around. The net result was that at two o'clock this morning, one of the members of the Governing Board called Mr. Richards from El Morocco and read him the letter. He also told Mr. Richards that he—the Governing Board member—had been asked by a columnist whether it was true that the Canteen was so completely split apart by internecine warfare that it was likely to be closed.

I suddenly saw why Tom had been so cheerful all along. It unrolled like a beautiful panorama, Jeff— the Iron Twain's carefully nurtured reputation for benevolence and patriotism, and the way the Sadler-Rabinowitz incident was going to sound after a mort of people had been discussing it with more enthusiasm than scientific detachment.

I closed my eyes in rapture.

"What hath God wrought!" I said to myself.

Mr. Richards broke in on my reflections by remarking that if I didn't consider it intrusive, he would like to know our plans.

I told him our plans.

"But you can't do that!" he said. "You don't belong at the Canteen any more."

"No, but we haven't fallen too low to use the United States mails."

"You're discredited. You left under a cloud. Nobody will believe you."

I tried not to laugh too happily.

"Would you care to take a chance on that?"

Surprisingly, Mr. Richards laughed, too.

"Where do you think you're going to get the addresses?" he asked indulgently.

"We already have them. A genie in a bottle got them for us."

If the Birdseye Products people know what they are about, they will look up Mr. Richards and take a lesson or two in quick freezing.

"I am to understand," said Mr. R., "that if Mrs. Sadler writes to this Jewess, you won't mail out your libelous assault on her character?"

"Yes."

"You realize, of course, that this is blackmail?"

"We think of it more as whitemail," I said. "A squeeze play, if you like."

I have to admit for Mr. Richards that in his passion for controlling things, he has not left out himself. His manner was devoid of emotion when he said that if Bonnie and Lucy and I would be at his office at three o'clock this afternoon, with the letters, he would have a note for us to give to Mae Rabinowitz.

I said that Lucy was sick and Bonnie was working, but that I would be there—complete with all extant copies of the libelous assault on Mrs. Sadler's character. Without any concluding formalities, Mr. Richards hung up.

Only one thing worries me, Skipper. I'm afraid that between now and my ultimate dissolution I'll never spend another interlude as blissful as the one that succeeded Mr. Richards' call. When I thought of how Mae was going to feel, I had to run and do a few entrechats up and down the hall. I'd have burst with a loud report, otherwise. I called Mae and Lucy, and we babbled wildly at each other. After leaving a message for Bonnie, I tried to settle down to the housework. I managed to restore our little tepee to a semblance of order, though a domestic science authority might have turned a jot queasy at some of my shortcuts.

It was about an hour later, while I was cleaning up the living room, that I had occasion to shake my duster out of the window. (I know it's against the law, but have the municipal legislators ever tried to shake a duster into the toilet?) It's a lovely spring day, and there was a flower wagon being colorful and urgent at the end of the block, so I stopped for a minute to contemplate the street. That was how I happened to notice the man coming along the sidewalk. May I not have naturally curly hair in my next incarnation if it wasn't Mr. Richards. I was so startled, I involuntarily exclaimed, "Hey!" (I wish I were such a perfect lady that ejaculations like "Huh?" and "Hey!" never escaped me, even in the most critical moments, but they do.)

Mr. Richards looked up. He stopped, transfixed, and stared. With three long strides, he disappeared into the vestibule and the doorbell rang. I disposed of the duster and my apron with lightning speed. By great good fortune, I'd already been out of doors, so I was properly dressed and my face was fixed up with the requisite number of brightly colored unguents. When I pressed the buzzer, I almost had a return of my former trepidation about Mr. R., until I remembered that we had him by the short hairs and besides, I was in my own house. Which makes a difference. When I opened the door, he stalked straight past me into the living room. He can be exquisitely mannerly, when he wants to, but he never bothers unless he can take it off his income tax.

178

Once in the living room, he stood still and looked around.

"Oh," he said. "Books."

"Yes," I replied demurely, following him in. "Do you read?"

He wheeled and looked at me.

"Just lips," he said.

I asked him how he happened to be passing our house, and he eyed me with austere displeasure and said coldly that he was coming away from Mrs. Sadler's. She lives, it seems, not far from us.

Relapsing into fretfulness, Mr. Richards added that he had walked five blocks trying to find a taxi. This did not seem to me cause for alarm, as in any army that traveled on its stomach, Mr. Richards would have a very soft thing.

"Won't you sit down?" I said.

But he seemed to prefer prowling around. He examined my potpourri vases and studied the lowboy as if it were on sale and he an embryo purchaser. That he had expected to find me living in a tenement, with coal in the bathtub and other stigmata of a "radical" household, was fairly obvious, and I realized with something of a shock that for all his wealth, prestige and power, in some ways he's a very inexperienced man. In the course of his wanderings he came to the pile of mimeographed letters on the typewriting table. He picked one up and glanced at the first page. Shuddering, he put it down again.

"Of course, she shouldn't have said it," he remarked

crossly, "but you've blown the thing up till it's all out of proportion."

I didn't answer. As long as we were going to get the note for Mae, there seemed to be no percentage in arguing with Mr. Richards about things he doesn't want to understand.

More agreeably, he continued, "I'll have to meet this Mae What's-her-name. From all the trouble you've taken over her, she must be a remarkable person."

"She isn't a bit remarkable."

Mr. Richards' face conveyed something akin to horror.

"She has a lovely smile, she's a marvelous dancer, and she knows what a Texas leaguer is. The servicemen like her a lot. But her figure is bad—she goes in at the waist, but she goes right out again—and she must certainly be the least original thinker on the Eastern seaboard. Also, she yells when she gets excited."

"Then why did you stir up all this trouble about her?" Mr. Richards asked angrily.

He answered his own question.

"For the sheer pleasure of making mischief. Of all the irresponsible . . . There's a war on. Don't you young women realize what you're doing?"

"If you don't sit down," I said, "people will think we aren't going steady any more."

Mr. Richards caught his breath, but decided not to laugh.

"Pain is pain," I said, "no matter to whom it happens. When somebody gets hurt, we don't stop and say, 'Well, if it isn't Noel Coward, it doesn't count.' "

Mr. Richards had been about to subside into a chair, but he changed his mind.

"You're a lawyer," I continued. "Presumably you know the Constitution almost by heart. Possibly the Declaration of Independence, too. But you've missed one of the main points of both of them."

I expected him to interrupt, but he didn't.

"They were both framed, in part," I said, "with the idea of eliminating unnecessary pain."

Mr. Richards' countenance was an object of interest, owing to the fact that a variety of emotions was trying to crowd into an area not usually inhabited by even one.

"Mae Rabinowitz will have enough heartaches if she just gets married and raises a family. It won't be necessary to give her any little extra, sadistic jabs on account of her religion. She'll find out it's a vale of tears, without any help from Mrs. Sadler."

"Nonsense!" exclaimed Mr. Richards. "I've told you before and I tell you again—those people aren't as sensitive as you think."

I remained silent.

"The Jews get along all right," Mr. Richards said defensively.

I laughed.

"How do you know?" I asked teasingly. "Did they take you into their confidence?"

Before he had time to answer, I went on, "Is that a

note from Mrs. Sadler you have in your pocket? Or is it just a paper napkin left over from a picnic?"

Mr. Richards put his hands in his pockets, tilted his head, raised his eyebrows, and in many other ways arranged himself to look quizzical.

"What makes you think I have a note from Mrs. Sadler?"

"You've just come from there, and at the Canteen they always say you're the only one who can make the old . . . who can persuade Mrs. Sadler to do anything against her will."

I regretted the statement instantly. It was, I thought, such a flagrant example of the old ooze that only a man coming out of ether would accept it without suspicion.

"M-m-m-m," said Mr. Richards.

Your sex—Geoffrey, old boy—ought not to be left alone in the same universe with women.

Mr. Richards fingered the contents of his breast pocket and drew out an envelope, which he tossed on the table.

I saw that the note was unsealed.

"May I read it?" I asked.

Mr. Richards nodded and picked up the pile of letters, which he clasped rather firmly.

Mrs. Sadler's note was graceful, evasive and insincere, but in a tenuous way it did qualify as an apology.

I looked at Mr. Richards.

"Mrs. Sadler never composed this herself," I said. "You must have dictated it."

"What makes you think so?"

"She wouldn't write this fluently. You can tell from the way she talks."

(It was hard for me to limit myself to such a niggling term as "fluent," since with me Mrs. Sadler's prose poem enjoyed the esteem usually reserved for the Song of Solomon.)

Mr. Richards riffled the mimeographed letters and indulged in an infinitesimal smile.

I pointed to the fireplace.

"Want to burn the letters?"

"Schoolgirl dramatics," he said, but he made no objection when I took the sheaf from his hands and tossed it across the andirons.

"You know how it is with us decayed gentlewomen," I said apologetically. "Anything for a bit of excitement."

From the table drawer, I extracted the typewritten original of the letters and put it on top of the pile. Spreading the papers out fanwise, so they'd burn faster, I touched a match to them. Mr. Richards and I stood side by side in front of the hearth and watched the flames.

When the letters were blazing beyond the possibility of salvage, Mr. Richards straightened up, squared his shoulders, and retrieved his hat from the lowboy. As he turned around, it was evident from the set of his face that the honeymoon was over.

"Let's have it quite clear," he said icily, "that this doesn't constitute a precedent. You're young, and much must be forgiven young people. But you've made a fuss over nothing and wasted a great deal of my time. Not to mention imperiling the very existence of the Canteen through the withdrawal of Mrs. Sadler's financial support."

The way in which he mentioned Mrs. Sadler caught my ear, and the knowledge flew along my veins that Mr. Richards had rather enjoyed making Mrs. Sadler write that note. But he wouldn't enjoy it a second time.

Mr. Richards went down the hall and let himself out. I followed him. Outside the door, he turned around. He was wearing his mordant little smile.

"Next time," he said, "I'll be cleverer."

I kissed the tips of my fingers and laid them quickly against his cheek.

"So will we," I answered, and closed the door.

And we will, too, Jeff. I burned the letters, but I didn't burn the envelopes.

Your correspondent, brother dear, is all worn out from the excitement and makes a motion that the meeting be adjourned. That's a piteous story about the soldier whose cot is right-hand cot to yours. Poor little tyke! Of course, what he really wants is for his faithless bride to be a better woman than she actually is, and the Red Cross can't fix that for him. He'll have to cut his losses, and I don't envy you the heart-rending job of tutoring him in it.

But will you permit me the merest fraction of a smile? I can't entirely dismiss from my mind the notion of what you would have answered, when you first went to Bragg, if anyone had said you would end up being legal adviser and father confessor to a musketeer who reads the comic magazines. I think it was extremely nice of him to take you on, considering the uninviting precision of your English.

Good-by for now, Dogface.

Love,
Gretchen

April 1st

Jeff, you peerless thing—

I'm so grateful that I haven't any words. Well, at any rate, I have only one word. If anyone should ask me to indicate a sweetie-pie *quick*, your name would rise instantly to my lips. The letter came this morning, and as soon as I saw how thick it was, I had a suspicion that Chevalier Jeff was galloping to the rescue.

What did you say to our venerable sire? Whatever it was, he didn't like it at first. When he started to read, his eyebrows shot up, and at the end of the second page he half rose from his chair—only when he saw me looking at him, he folded up again. While he finished the letter, his face just sat on the front of his skull and did nothing, and he departed for the office without comment. But he came home early. I was in the living room, creating those lumps and puckers I try to dignify with the name of mending. (Or is it a painful memory?) That it was an important occasion I realized when I saw that Father was carrying an

185

enormous florist's box. The Progenitor has heard that blossoms sometimes get broken, in which case the Salvation Army looks after them, but he is not one to acknowledge that they also exist unimpaired.

Father put the box on the sofa, inspected himself in the mirror over the mantel, and tightened the knot in his tie.

"My son," he said, "instructs me to stop looking ten years older."

I arrived without loss of time against his coat lapels. "Oh, Father!"

He kissed the top of my head and then held me away from him.

"Open the box," he said, giving me one of those punitive wallops across the shoulder that make the old man's tenderness indistinguishable from a fast game of lacrosse.

They were spring flowers, and there were so many of them that I was half afraid to lift them up, for fear there might be a dead gangster underneath.

"You must have spent a fortune!" I exclaimed. "Just an olive branch would have done."

"No," Father said. "There had to be enough to bury the hatchet."

I took hold of his hand.

"There are."

Father gave a tired sigh.

"My boy Geoffrey," he announced, with melancholy pride, "certainly doesn't mince words."

"He didn't get that," I said, laughing, "from the

distaff side"—at which Father looked startled and pleased.

I went to fetch urns and receptacles, and Father got the news on the radio. Jockeying flowers around in a vase is one of my favorite pursuits, and it was lovely to have concord and amity restored to our rooftree, so I was very happy. But it was a sober kind of felicity, Jeff. Father hasn't entirely obeyed your injunction to stop looking ten years older. I think he was getting fed up with his strenuous imitation of the polar icecap, and he's grateful to you for resolving the situation for him. I know, though—and I think he does, too—that he and I will never go back to exactly our old footing. Tom Garrett has been telling me ever since he came here that I ought to learn to regard Father as a fallible human being, but until Father went to Janie about Will Greene, I didn't know what Tom was talking about. I do now. It seems odd to say that it's exciting, but in a curious way, it is. Only it hurts to have to hurt Father, and I wish parents would come like curtains and shirts—pre-shrunk. However, I suppose you can't have everything, though my instinctive response to this sentiment is always, "Why not?"

But here I am complaining when—thanks to you, my dearly cherished relative—not only is Father darkening my door again, but Deborah is out of hock. Before I had finished arranging Father's flowers, Janie called me. She was sullen and disagreeable, and only asked me if I could come to lunch tomorrow, hanging up as soon as I said yes. Nevertheless, remembering

187

the long and bootless years Bill has spent trying to get her to speak to his sister, I wasn't prepared to quibble at a little ungraciousness. How did you do it, Jeffie? I know you're a born strategist, and if it hadn't been for your fine Italian hand—young as you were. too— I'd still be an unsalaried attendant in Philip's self-starting lunatic asylum. But even in the throes of an infatuation, I haven't got Janie's streak of immutable stubbornness.

It's all a wonder and a wild surmise. Not surprisingly, the subject of Janie made Father guiltily self-conscious, so I didn't like to dwell on it; but apparently she called him up in tears when she got your letter, and Father said she was so shocked and startled she was almost hysterical. Apparently, also, Father did what he could to call her off. But it seems to have been your letter that broke the British square, though all Father ventured was that you had been "extremely impatient." I try to visualize our gentle Geoffrey being "extremely impatient," but I can only conclude that association with the sergeants of a line outfit has made you query the effectiveness of subtlety and finesse. It makes me realize how much I want to see you again. In the meantime, we are all—even Janie, I suspect—a-swim with gratitude that you have straightened us out, and when we want to bring lines into our faces, we allow ourselves to realize that you might have been born into somebody else's family.

I keep promising you, Bro., that my letters are going

to be reassuring and tranquil—and then promptly dispatching a complicated outcry of pain, anguish and frustration. But this time I think I'm really going to keep the promise, because it seems as if all the parts of my life which appeared to have taken wing, have now come back. Only each of them is changed and modified and altered. Of this generalization, the most signal example has yet to be related. If you can put up with just a little bit more of my unconquerable addiction to the first person singular, I'll tell you about it. (After that, I'll learn some other pronouns. I hear there's quite a selection.)

After Mr. Richards had departed yesterday morning, leaving the note for Mae, life seemed a much more appetizing way to spend the time than it had before he telephoned. I began to wonder whether apologizing to Tom was, after all, so inconceivable. Father was going to Mr. Howell's for dinner, so I didn't have to do any shopping, and after downing a morsel of lunch, I had a bath, did my nails, washed and ironed the collar of my blue dress, and took other steps designed to give me that mixture of crispness and opulence so admirably characterized by the Fig Newton. Tom, however, didn't come in till nine o'clock in the evening, by which time I was noticeably wilted and, to put it mildly, over-rehearsed.

When I heard his key in the lock, I was trying to read a detective story which I had swooped out to the rental library to secure, in the hope that it would give me poise, detachment and perspective. Tom started to go right to his room without speaking to me, but I called him. He came into the living room.

"Oh," he said, in pretended surprise, "it's the little Gentile-baiter."

I had thought I'd figured out every possible thing he could say, but this cut the ground out from under me so completely that my head rocked. My mind was a spinning blank, and I couldn't do anything but sit and listen to my heart pound.

There was a long and nerve-searing silence, before Tom said politely, "Did you want me for anything?"

In desperation I got up, snatched Mrs. Sadler's note from the table, and silently proffered it to him.

He looked surprised, but he opened it and read it. Carefully restoring it to the envelope, he handed it back.

"Very interesting," he said.

By this time it was overwhelmingly evident that the apology project was a failure of classic proportions, and it only remained for me to keep the tears in my eyes from spilling over until he had turned his back and started out. But he didn't go. He kept on standing there. My vision was too much blurred to read the expression on his face, even if I could have gotten my eyes off the floor.

At length I said miserably, "I'm sorry."

"It's quite all right."

"Don't be such a liar!" I said angrily, looking up and abandoning any pretense that I wasn't crying.

"When you say it that way, you mean exactly the opposite. You mean it isn't all right, at all."

"I mean exactly what I said," he replied coldly. "If you want to spend the rest of your life falling in love with a series of degenerate tootsie-rolls like Philip, it's your privilege. It *is* quite all right."

"At least," he added, "as far as I'm concerned."

I groped back of me toward the table and got my handkerchief. By that time, I could have used a mainsail.

"But I don't!" I cried, my utterance somewhat impeded by crumpled cloth.

Tom looked skeptical.

"You're so cruel," I said chokingly. "How can you be so cruel?"

"I'm not cruel, Gretchen. I only seem that way to you because you're so unnaturally wary of men. Of most men, anyway. All the ones that aren't blackguards."

This had a truthful echo about it, but I was in no shape to think clearly.

"I said I was sorry. What more can I do?"

"You shouldn't have bothered to say it. Because you're not."

I stopped in the middle of a sob to stare at him.

"You've been suspicious and distrustful of me right from the beginning," Tom said. "You keep looking here, there and everywhere for some way to 'handle' me. So far it hasn't crossed your icebound little mind that maybe I'm not supposed to be 'handled.' "

He fished in his pocket, got out a key ring, and started twirling it round on his finger.

"Your trouble," he said, "is that you've always got to be the boss. It always has to be your show. Look at tonight, for instance. You're all dressed up, and you had this interview completely planned out. You were going to be so full of cute sayings that I'd let you off lightly."

He detached the key ring from his finger and dropped it back into his pocket.

"Why should I let you off lightly? You made a grossly insulting remark in a situation where it was entirely uncalled for."

What kept me from fainting was the certain knowledge that Tom would just have left me there, walked out, and told the nearest buzzards that he could put them on to a good thing.

"You've always," Tom was saying, when the room came back to its moorings, "been too damned cute for your own good."

"I didn't mean to say it," I whispered. "I don't know why I said it."

"Don't you? I do. That remark was the Big Push. It was your last, anguished attempt to get the whip hand."

My handkerchief dropped to the floor, but I had no further use for it.

"What was supposed to happen when you said it?" Tom asked. "I was supposed to be utterly crushed. I was supposed to slink away with my self-respect in tatters. Either I'd go away altogether, or—what you hoped—I'd stay here and let you use your alleged physical distaste for me as a club to keep me in line."

The palms of my hands were soaking wet, but my mouth was so dry I couldn't get my lips together.

"I'm a courtly fellow," Tom said genially. "Since you want the whip hand so badly, I'm willing to give it to you. Do you want me to leave, Gretchen?"

I almost sank to my knees with the pang that went through me.

"Do you want me to leave? All you have to do is say yes."

Frantically, I thought about running away, but I couldn't move.

Tom was inexorable.

"Just nod your head, if you can't speak."

A drop of perspiration detached itself from my temple and moved with agonizing deliberation down the side of my cheek.

"There won't be any hard feelings."

Tom's voice was persuasive.

"I'm perfectly willing to go. After all, it isn't your fault if you find me physically repulsive."

"I don't," I gasped. "I don't."

"Well!"

He took a step toward me and stopped.

"That," he said, "is going to make your life a whole lot simpler."

After a moment's reflection, he went into the hall and came back with his topcoat over his arm.

"I have to go out and buy a man a drink," he said. "A physically attractive specimen called Tom Garrett."

At the door he paused.

"I'm going to the country tomorrow. I'll be gone before you're up."

He adjusted a fold in the topcoat.

"Doctor's orders," he said apologetically. "Some friends of mine are digging a garden, and I need exercise for my arm. I'll be back in three or four days."

He closed the door carefully behind him.

I crept to my room. The next thing I knew it was three o'clock in the morning. And although I discovered that I had fallen asleep with my clothes on and the light burning, it was not an unhappy awakening.

Love,
Gretchen

P.S. I didn't mean to conclude so brusquely, but after Tom's intensive overhauling of my verbal habits, I'm afraid to say anything for fear it might be construed as cute. I'll only . . .

No, that's cute, too.

P.P.S. How is the poor little tyke getting along?

April 3rd

Jeff, darling—

Only one night! The Army ought to have its head examined. Don't they understand that your character is not only beautiful, but intricate? Don't they realize that you're much too imposingly complex to be properly savored in a single evening? On the other hand, perhaps—after all—they know best. The sooner you get to this atoll or land mass where you are billed for a personal appearance, the sooner you'll be back. If it were done when 'tis done, then 'twere well it were done quickly.

Oh, Jeff, it's going to be so delicious to see you again! The joyful dither to which your family has succumbed would suggest to a casual observer that we had won the Irish Sweepstakes. Janie squealed when I told her the news, and completely forgot to be haughty as we made plans for serving lollipops and cough drops all next week and pooling our ration points to get you a stalled ox. Bill and Janie and Deborah will come down to dinner, and Father and I will meet you at the train. You don't mind being knocked over in the Pennsylvania Station, do you? Because when it comes to greeting you, I'm likely to have my mind on my work. Or do you think the M.P.'s would be stuffy about it?

As to Father, he's so proud of you, and so excited about seeing you again, that he's having a little trouble containing his emotion within the limits of a single epidermis. Unless you can contrive to do something disgraceful, I'm rather afraid the Progenitor is going to give at the seams. He wants me, by the way, to ask you whether you want to go to the theater after dinner or whether you'd prefer to stay home and have your words hung on. In the event that you want to go to the theater, you are to say which of the current masques you'd like to witness.

Tom's arm is almost healed, and I think he'll be out on a trip by the time you get here. I'm disappointed that you won't meet him, but glad we'll be just a family gathering and that you'll have your own room to sleep in. Bill made the brilliant suggestion that we shouldn't let Aunt Julie know you're coming. After you've gone, we'll tell her you arrived without notice and surprised us. Even at that, she'll be outraged that we didn't call her up. But soldiers, confronted by Aunt Julie's theory that they are only fighting for the carriage trade, have been known to take off for the North woods—leaving a note for the enemy that they'd find cold meat and salad in the icebox.

When you come home, Jeff, it's going to be all fun and games—balloons for the kiddies and beautiful nautch girls to wash your back. There won't be much time to talk, so I thought I'd like to tell you something that is, perhaps, better written than spoken anyway. You're shipping out, and nobody—I guess—can come between a man and his contemplation of imminent peril. But we'd like you to know that if you get killed, you'll have all the immortality that is ours to bestow. As long as we are alive—Janie and Bill and Deborah, and Father and I—you will always be the Special One. You will always be the one who rose to the bitterest discipline of all, and ours will be a long, unceasing pride that we produced you and that you were one of us.

I suppose, though, you are no exception to the general rule that soldiers worry more about being maimed than getting killed. We promise you nothing can happen to you that your family isn't equal to. There's no way you could be hurt, however unbeautifully, that would make you any less our unique, individual Jeff. If you have to make your life over again from the bottom—or what seems like the bottom— we'll be there every step of the way. We'll be proud to be. And when you're afraid, darling, remember that whatever happens to you, will happen to other soldiers, too. You won't be alone, Jeff, believe me.

But two paragraphs of solemnity are more than enough. Anyway, I expect our main problem will be how we're going to keep you down on the farm, after you've seen Paree. And in the meantime, we have a night and part of a day in which to show you what the American Home can do in the way of food, drink and cheery badinage when it's really humping itself. Be sure to write and tell us anything special you want. I will get some jelly beans for you to bring to Deborah. She thinks of you so exclusively as a purveyor of that commodity, that they are now known among her habitual associates as jeffy beans.

On that ominous note, I will bring this to a close.

Love,
Gretchen

P.S. I note with pleasure that the Southern lieutenant has turned up again. I was going to let his disquisition lie fallow until you got here, but it occurs to me that you have never mentioned what part of the Army he inhabits and perhaps he isn't shipping out with you. The lieutenant's argument—stripped of the circumlocutions which make it suitable for a lady's ear—seems to be that the Negroes on his father's farm ought not to vote, because they have more sexual intercourse than you can shake a stick at. Does the lieutenant think he is taking me by surprise? I knew *something* was making those people happy . . .

I often think, Jeff, that what makes it difficult for the American Negro to adjust to the land of the free is not only the discrimination, but the contradictions in the white man's attitude. In wartime, the darker brother is supposed to be such a bad fighter he can only be used in labor battalions; but in peacetime he is supposed to be such a formidable opponent that he has to be kept ruthlessly in subjection, because if he ever got started, nobody would be able to withstand him. The contradiction about Negro sexuality must be even more puzzling to them. We make it very clear that because of something over which they have no control—the color of their skin—they aren't good enough to work, fight, worship, eat, vote, dance or go to school with us. Then in the next breath we turn around and bawl them out for not observing the moral standards of a society we have just told them they don't belong to.

I once asked Tom whether it's true, as most people

seem to believe, that Negroes have more sex life than white people. He said he didn't know, but he would think so.

"There's a thing called primitive sexuality," he said, "which means that the way to be good in bed is to live so simply you haven't any bed to be good in."

"We reserve all the interesting and stimulating jobs for ourselves," he said. "As well as the best schools and school systems for our own children, and the best houses in the best parts of town for our own families."

He shrugged.

"A man has to do something with his energy. It doesn't just evaporate, like water."

On another occasion, when we were talking about race, he observed that there is nothing like keeping up the payments on an electric washing machine to make a person temperate and chaste.

"At the risk of disillusioning you, Gretchen," he said, "it must be admitted that a good deal of what the white man thinks of as his instinctive chastity is really nothing nobler than fatigue."

At any rate, Jeff, if you accept the lieutenant's description of his father's farm hands—which I do—it certainly doesn't seem as if their vote would be a thoughtful and considered enterprise. But what about their children and grandchildren? The Negroes the lieutenant is talking about are grown up. They probably wouldn't change much, even if he wanted them to, because adults usually don't. It's in the rising generations of Negroes that the lieutenant's oppor-

tunity lies, if he wants to use it. He has another opportunity in his own children and grandchildren. Is he
going to teach them the old tradition, verbatim, or is
he going to break it down a little, so that they in their
turn can break it down a little more?

Has the lieutenant got any plans for the young
Negroes and the young whites? And if he has, will he
stick to them? Or will he give them up the first time
his maiden aunts put the screws on him, and just take
it all out in worrying? I think his resentment is justi-
fied, when Northerners who haven't got a farmful of
Negro field hands outside the doorstep make free with
unsolicited advice. On the other hand, the lieutenant
has to expect that when he doesn't plan and act himself, he tempts other people beyond their strength to
plan and act for him. And you tell him for me that he
is not to take the easy way out and go around saying
Negroes are children. Because what is the main char-
acteristic of all children, anywhere? They grow up.
You can't stop them. There's never been but one
Peter Pan, and if the lieutenant isn't more discreet,
the estate of Sir James M. Barrie will sue him.

As to your own part of the letter, Bro., I bet you I
have talked to as many white-supremacy boys as you
have. I've had them roar at me, and been splashed
with the foam from their lips. Nor do I think anyone
going into battle has ever been much more scared than
I, when I've been sitting with a Negro boy at the Canteen and have observed the screaming South bearing

down on me. You can tell them twenty yards away. But in these situations, the instinct of self-preservation generally helps you to find a way out. My own desire not to play jump center in a race riot inspired me to take a leaf from the w.-s. boys' own book. I talk to them the way they talk to visiting Northerners who express distaste about the "For White Only" signs in the South.

"That's the way we do things around here," I say nastily, "and if you know what's good for you, you won't meddle."

It isn't the prettiest conversational gambit in the world, but it makes them respect you. With those babies, it's important to git thar fustest and beat them at their own game. (Some day one of them is going to say, "But I *don't* know what's good for me." To date, mercifully for me, they haven't thought of it.)

It seems to me, Skipper, that you have to realize the white-supremacy boys are spoiled children. "I want MY way," they scream, and like all spoiled children, they advance no justification for it except that it *is* their way. But the most formidable brat, in the long run, is no match for a really wise adult. The adult is cleverer, and has more staying power. I think the point is not that the white-supremacy boys are brattish. I think it's a question of how experienced and courageous and mature the people are who don't believe in white supremacy. That's why I keep saying that the thing for you to think of is not what shocking things you see and hear in the South, but what you are going to do yourself when you get back to the North.

Before I went to the Canteen—gosh, you must be tired of that clause!—I always used to think of the Negroes as a passive mass about which I was going to do something benign but unspecified some day when I got around to it. But after you've met and worked with a variety of them, you come to see very quickly that no solution of the race problem is possible without their active co-operation and good will. It's been our experience that most Negroes are willing to go more than halfway with white people in whose good faith they believe. But how can they believe in our good faith, Jeff, if we don't demonstrate it? How, in fact, can we believe in it ourselves?

April 5th

Sweet Caporal:

I've just realized—with no more of a jolt than I would sustain from a personal contribution to an electric circuit—that from now on I'll have to write to you on V-mail paper. To a correspondent as incurably expansive as I, this has all the earmarks of a hardship. So—though I ought by rights to be telephoning absentee Junior Hostesses and telling them to come on in, the war effort's fine—I decided to have one last fling on regular typewriting paper in unlimited quantities.

The reverberations from l'affaire Rabinowitz are

beginning to die down. The captains sent post cards to all the Junior Hostesses who signed the letter to Mrs. Sadler, saying that their signatures had been instrumental in securing an apology for Mae and that the captains wanted to thank them for their loyalty to a fellow worker and their willingness to take a stand against prejudice. The news created a sensation at the Canteen. I can't claim that creating a sensation at the Canteen is a Herculean task, since it can be done merely by cracking your knuckles. But the institution rocked with the story, and some of the garbled versions of it were sufficiently ingenious and picturesque to be worth the attention of a scenario writer.

A few unleavened souls—mostly Mrs. Sadler's protégées or would-be protégées—murmured that she had never said it and it was all an advertising scheme put over by a bunch of kikes. Most of the Canteen workers, however, went around with the buoyant step and beaming eye of people who have just come into money. Mrs. Sadler—the rich, the unassailable, the highly publicized—had been successfully challenged by, of *all* improbable people, the Junior Hostesses! Sic semper tyrannis. The rain falls upon the just and the unjust, but the moon shines down on pretty Left-Wing—to lapse into Mr. Richards' terminology.

Mae went back to the Canteen the night before last. I wasn't there, but Bonnie was, and she said dozens and dozens of Junior Hostesses told Mae they were glad to see her back, and added curiously, "What did the letter say?"

Instructed by Bonnie, Mae replied that Mrs. Sadler had just said she was sorry.

A few of the more impulsive J. H.'s went out and bought Mae a corsage. Mae was in the lobby when they gave it to her, and they were all chirping and lilting in female fashion when the Gravy Twain, giving the Canteen its usual evening once-over-heavily, arrived at the inner door. The Twain hove to and inspected the group of girls, who did not notice them. Mrs. Sadler's eye fell on Mae's corsage.

"Her birthday," Mrs. S. adjudged.

Mr. Richards nodded carelessly, and they turned away.

Bonnie said the temptation was almost irresistible to tell Mrs. Sadler that this was the girl to whom she had sent the note. It would have tempted me about as much as moving into a leper colony, but Bonnie doesn't want to stagnate, whereas I do. At any rate, Bonnie said nothing—feeling that there was no use antagonizing Mrs. Sadler unnecessarily, since we'll no doubt have to hold that tiger again before the troops come home.

Yesterday afternoon Bonnie and Lucy and I had our own celebration for the successful termination of the Rabinowitz affair. I had asked them over, thinking that we'd have a cup of tea and preen ourselves gently on having done our civic duty. But before the water began to boil, Tom came in, and in his customary fashion, changed the direction of things.

When I introduced him to Lucy, he blinked. Men

who can see well enough to find their way around without a cane always do. But it was Bonnie to whom he took an instant and especial liking, which was reciprocated. They're two of a kind. Dauntless. Though from any situation in which they were on opposing sides, a well-advised person would make a swift, informal exit.

Tom said that mental hospitals are full of people who have suffered complete nervous breakdowns from trying to celebrate on tea, so he went out and bought liquor and made Martinis. Bonnie had just proposed a toast to him—"You're the prettiest," she said, at which he shot me a look not unfreighted with significance—when the doorbell rang. It was Mae, come to get her note from Mrs. Sadler and to bring me a present. (She has presents for Bonnie and Lucy, too, but of course she didn't know she'd find them here.) Tom poured her a drink, and we settled down to an exuberant and relaxing post-mortem, of which an interesting feature was Lucy's modest disclaimer when Mae said the suicide squad was wonderful.

"It was nothing," Lucy replied. "We did it for the wife and kiddies"—a descent into vulgar parlance which ought to be commemorated on the tombstone of whoever invented the Martini.

Mae and Lucy left, in a little while, but Bonnie stayed and had another cocktail. She isn't used to cocktails, and it made her talkative; but Bonnie's talk is supple, salty and invigorating, and gives people the zestful feeling so convincingly set forth in the hymns of praise to Sal Hepatica. At last Bonnie had to go, too, and what happened then took me by surprise. It had seemed to me that Tom and I, addressing each other, had been as restrained and unchummy as a brace of bank examiners, but when the three of us converged on the door, Bonnie put one arm around Tom and the other around me.

"I'm going out and burn a candle to the Virgin," she said. "I'm going to tell her to lean over from the altar and say to you two, 'Why don't you come up some time?' "

Tom gave her a quick, attentive glance.

"I'm sending you home in a taxi," he said, and bundled her out while she was still saying good-by to me over her shoulder.

He must be better at finding cabs than Mr. Richards, because he was back before I had even decided whether my hair looked all right. He came straight over and—with, I noticed, an air of great dexterity—scooped me up in his good arm. Tipping my head back with a forefinger, he said, "Why don't you come up some time, Gretchen?"

So I said I would.

I'll tell you the rest when I see you. After Bill and Janie have taken their sleeping Delectable home, and after Father has gone to bed, you can run your head under the radiator—or whatever it is you do to get your hair so mussed when you're taking your ease. Then you can stretch out on the sofa, and I will take

off my shoes and sit on my feet in the red chair, and we
will really talk.

Hurry *up*.

Affectionately,
Gretchen